WINTER'S FALL

by

Sarah Land

"...And the flood was forty days upon the earth; and the waters increased, and bare up the ark...And all flesh died that moved upon the earth, both fowl, and of cattle, and of beast, and of every creeping thing that creepeth upon the earth, and every man: All in whose nostrils was the breath of life..."

Genesis Chapter 7

Prologue
November

You never forget your first dead body. I knew I never would. The look on her face would be forever burned into my retinas. In her lifeless eyes I could see her fear—fear of death and of the one who had done this to her—but I could also see hope. It was the hope I saw in her eyes—hope that someone would come in time to save her—that would haunt me. Because I hadn't.

I let go of her shoulder and scrambled away. I wanted to run from the corpse at my feet, to give into the insanity hovering at the periphery of my consciousness. But I couldn't, I needed to find Justin. Still, I could feel a scream building in my throat. But before I let it escape someone grabbed me roughly from behind, and covered my mouth with their hand. I thrashed about violently, trying to get out of the arms that were around me, but whoever was behind me was strong, and

I couldn't get away from their iron grip.

Chapter 1
August

"Winter, aren't you listening?"

I looked up from the lunch I had been focused on eating, and stared innocently at Amanda. Amanda Perdue had strawberry blonde hair, fair skin and emerald green eyes, which on anyone else would have looked gorgeous, but somehow on Amanda seemed unattractive. It was as if all you saw when you looked at her was how she saw herself. Now her green eyes were watching me, not as though she were upset or annoyed, but as if she *hoped* I had been listening.

I hadn't been listening, and the truth was I had stopped really listening to her a couple of days ago. It wasn't that she wasn't nice—she was—and I appreciated her kindness more than she would ever know. However, all she ever talked about was Thomas McGregor and how wonderful he was. To be honest, I really didn't see what she liked about him. He seemed like a tool to me. He was obviously just using Amanda for her English homework, but it's not like I could tell Amanda that. I mean, who was I to judge? I had only known either one of them for a little over a week.

In the month since I had moved to Salem, Missouri, I had learned that it was one of those small towns that was just large enough that no one ever had to leave, but small enough that everyone knew everyone else's business. Most of the kids at school had known each other since they were in diapers. Then there was me, the new kid. I preferred to keep my business to myself. So, naturally, rumors spread about me. The topic of most of these rumors being my unusual circumstances: I am an emancipated sixteen-year-old with my own apartment. Apparently, there aren't many of those around here. Imagine that. I'm not sure what sort of glamorous life I was assumed to have, but before school had even started, it had earned me an invitation to an end of the summer party. I had never been to a party that didn't involve party hats and birthday cake, so of course I went.

It didn't take long for me to figure out that the party scene wasn't my thing, but it didn't matter. It took even less time for them to realize that my life wasn't as exciting as they had hoped.

The truth is this, my mother, Paige Loveless, has always been highly superstitious, believing in signs, omens, and horoscopes. Growing up, whenever she would get a bad feeling about a place we would move. We moved a lot. I didn't mind though, because as nice as every place had been, none of them had ever felt like home.

I never knew my father. I once saw a picture of him, though. My mother had been writing in her diary when an old Polaroid had fallen out. I noticed the man in the picture had gray eyes like mine, but then the picture was snatched away, never to be seen again. One glimpse was all I had of him, but I didn't mind.

I idolized my mother. I wanted to be just like her. When I was nine my mother and I took a trip to Las Vegas, because she said she was feeling lucky. By that time, I was used to her *feelings*, and I didn't think much of them. But when she won, it confirmed to me that she was magic.

Until then, my mother had worked a number of odd jobs: waitress, cashier, even flight attendant. After our trip to Vegas, she never worked again. My mom never told me how much she had won, but it was enough to support our rootless lifestyle, which was comfortable though not extravagant.

I continued believing my mother was magic until puberty set in. Then everything changed. All those quirky things I used to love about her, I suddenly hated. I didn't want to be unusual or different anymore. I just wanted to be normal. I wanted to fit in, but it wasn't meant to be.

Right after I turned fourteen, my enigmatic mother decided to emancipate me. She told me that if anything ever happened to her, she didn't want the court deciding my fate. I was used to her unusual habits, and though I didn't like it, there was nothing I could really do about it. Unbeknownst to me, she also made me the executor of her life trust, and had given me the power of attorney over her medical decisions.

I didn't find out about that until the doctors approached me at the hospital shortly after my mom had been in the accident.

My mother had always talked about returning to Salem, where she had grown up. So, six months later when my mother still hadn't come out of her coma, and the doctors asked which long-term care facility I wished to put her in, I took her home. Looking back, sometimes I wonder if she knew. Maybe she was magic after all.

Salem Residential Care is a friendly nursing home, located right off the highway, next to the small area hospital. They were glad to take my mom, even though she is much younger than their usual patients. She has her own private room, which I had painted yellow—her favorite color.

When school started, everyone was talking about me, but no one was exactly talking to me. That's when Amanda had approached me, and offered to let me sit with her in the cafeteria.

"Winter Loveless, I said are you listening?" Amanda said again, pulling me from my thoughts.

"Sorry, I was distracted. What were you saying?" I asked, taking another bite of my spaghetti, and wondering why anyone ever complained about school food.

"Thomas said hi to me today. I was sitting in English class this morning, minding my own business, and *he* came over and talked to *me*. I've been smiling ever since," Amanda said.

"That's great," I said, forcing a smile. She was talking about Thomas again. Ugh!

"You moved here from Denver, didn't you?"

"Littleton, actually, but yes."

"So, did you have a boyfriend there?" Amanda asked, sipping her milk dreamily.

"No."

11

"Why not? You're gorgeous."

I felt myself blush and regarded my reflection in the window behind her. My gray eyes stared back at me. I wouldn't call myself gorgeous, and I didn't think anyone else would either. It's not that I'm ugly. I even have some good features. But the sum of my parts makes me look average at best.

"Amanda, boys stopped paying any attention to me about the time that the other girls our age developed curves, and I remained flat as a pancake."

"Your body isn't that bad. If you were taller you'd look like a runway model," Amanda said.

"Yeah, well I'm not tall."

"I'd trade with you any day. I hate being tall. When you're short, it's cute. You're petite. I, on the other hand, look like Gumby," Amanda said.

12

This got a real smile from me. "You don't look like Gumby."

I was scrutinizing my reflection in the window, trying to see myself as Amanda did, when I saw him and my heart stopped.

He was outside at a table with two of the most beautiful girls I had ever seen in my life. His hair was dark and silky, though longer than I remembered, hanging just long enough to brush his collar. His skin still held the remnants of his summer tan, and his eyes, though turned away from me, I knew were an intense chocolate brown than nearly disappeared beneath his thick black lashes.

Justin Smith laughed at something the gorgeous blonde next to him said before he turned to listen to the tall, black haired beauty across the table from him. Mesmerized, I watched the flow of the muscles in his back and neck as he moved and spoke, and I felt my heart restart with an irregular fluttering that quickly spread to my stomach.

"Who are they?" I asked.

Amanda looked over her shoulder. "Oh, that's Carrie Sullivan and Brittany Rainwater. They're seniors and are the most popular girls at the school. They both moved here a couple of years ago—Carrie from somewhere in California, and Brittany from New Mexico—and they became fast friends. Janie Roberts and Becca Howard hated it. Becca graduated last year, so you probably never met her, but she and Janie used to rule around here. Then Carrie and Brittany showed up, and instantly took over. When it was obvious they couldn't compete, Becca and Janie tried to incorporate themselves into Brittany and Carrie's group, but it didn't work. No, Carrie and Brittany are a clique of two, and they like it that way.

Personally, I don't see what the big deal is. Sure, they're beautiful and all, but so is Janie. But that's the way things go. Some people have just got it—whatever *it* is.

Sitting with them is Justin Smith. He's in our grade, and just as untouchable. Janie's had her eyes on him for years, but hasn't been able to land him yet. Who knows maybe this year...

Whatever else Amanda was saying I didn't hear. I knew who Justin Smith was. I just never expected to see him here.

I pushed my tray away. There was no way I was going to be able to eat anything else.

An eternity later, I tore my eyes away from Justin, and turned my attention back to Amanda, who seemed oblivious to the recent detour my attention had taken. I forced my eyes to remain on Amanda as she once again began talking about

Thomas, but I was acutely aware of every movement Justin

made. When he got up and left, my heart wanted to follow.

Chapter 2

My mom and I never had much money, but the summer before I turned six must have been a particularly tough one. That summer my mom sent me to live with Justin's family so she could pick up more shifts at work. Elaine Smith, Justin's mom, had been friends with my mom since the two of them were in high school, though I'd never met her. And, as a favor to my mom, she had agreed to watch me.

So, that June, my Mom dropped me off at the Smith's. Within minutes she was gone, and I was being herded to the back yard to play. And that's where I met Justin.

His dark hair had been buzzed short for the summer, and he was wearing nothing but a pair of blue Bermuda shorts. He was digging in the dirt, which I remember looked like fun, but I was angry at my mom for leaving me with total strangers, and wasn't about to admit it. Instead, I took out my anger on the boy in front of me. I remember saying something like, "Only stupid people dig in the dirt." Then Justin looked up from the hole he had just finished digging, and I instantly regretted my hateful words. His dark intense eyes had me mesmerized even then, and I began calling myself names in my head, mentally beating myself up for being so rude to the only person I had to play with for the next three months. And while I was trying to think of some way to take it back, to make amends, a clod of dirt came sailing through the air, nailing me right in the face. And that is how we spent the rest of the summer—Justin hitting me or throwing things at me when he thought he could get away with it, and me making snide comments back to him.

Justin's parents weren't too bad, and I spent as much time as I could with them. But they were continually forcing me to spend time with Justin, who wanted nothing more than to make my life miserable. By the time August came around, and my mom came back for me, I was willing to forgive her anything if she would just take me away.

But I wouldn't have been so quick to forgive if I'd known what she was planning. The arrangement had worked out so well, that before I knew it, it had become an annual thing. That summer was just the first of many summers I'd spend with Justin.

The next summer Justin's family was staying at a beach house. When my mom dropped me off, I was determined to be friends with Justin. But the dynamic of our relationship was already set. All summer Justin smashed my sandcastles, pushed me into the surf when I least expected it, and slapped my incredibly sunburned shoulders. Still that year I did manage to keep the majority of my angry comments to myself, choosing to suffer his abuse in silence in an attempt to start fresh, but it seemed he had already made up his mind about me.

When we were seven we spent the summer at a cabin by a lake somewhere in the Rocky Mountains. If I thought the previous summer was bad, this one was worse. The first day I was there, Justin pushed me into the lake, and I nearly drowned. They managed to get all the water out of my lungs, but I came down with something that kept me in bed for the next three weeks. By the time I was well, I was so lonely that I was even looking forward to fighting with Justin. Unfortunately, there was a boy a couple of years older than us staying in a neighboring cabin, and the two of them ignored me for the rest of the summer. I though Justin hated me until one night, toward the end of August. I was heading for bed when he stopped me in the hall and gave me a Baby Ruth. He had gotten the candy bar earlier that week when he and his father had gone into the nearest town to get groceries, and had been parading it around. After handing it to me, he said he was sorry, smiled at me, and continued down the hall to his own room. I went home the next morning, never knowing what exactly he had apologized for.

The next summer I was afraid to face him. Although our relationship wasn't exactly the closest, I realized that because I was constantly moving and changing schools, Justin was the only long-term friend I had ever had. He was my best friend, and I didn't want him to ignore me again. That summer we stayed at an old plantation in Georgia that had been transformed into a resort. When I arrived, Justin actually looked happy to see me, and offered to let me play with him. We spent the next hour spying on the other guests in the lobby pretending we were secret agents. For the rest of the summer

Justin and I were inseparable. When September came, it was the first time I was sad to see the summer end.

The last summer I spent with Justin was when we were nine. His family was staying at the same beach house we had stayed at when we were six. When I found Justin sitting on the beach after my mom had dropped me off, I half expected him to throw sand at me the way he had the last time we were there, but he didn't. He made room for me to sit on the blanket next to him, and we picked up where we had left off the previous summer.

Sitting there beside him, watching the waves come rolling in again and again, I remember wondering why I had never noticed the gold flecks in Justin's dark eyes or the perfect shape of his lips. Every day I noticed more things about him, like how funny he was and how strong he was. It wasn't until one day when his hand brushed against mine that

I realized that I was in love with him. Every day was like a pleasant torture after that. I loved and hated every minute we had together.

I wanted to tell him how I felt, but was afraid of losing my best friend. So, I kept my mouth shut and told myself it was better that way. But then, at the end of the summer, when I was saying goodbye, I kissed him. It was a surprise even to me. One minute I was shaking his hand, and the next I was leaning in pressing my lips to his cheek. For one blissful moment I was happier than I'd even been in my life, but then I realized what I'd done and I freaked out and ran away. I'd ruined everything. Justin and I were finally getting along, but after that, I was sure he'd never want to speak to me again. I wished I could take it back, or at least apologize, but I left before I ever got the chance.

A few months later, my mom and I went to Vegas, and I never saw Justin or his family again.

Until now.

Chapter 3

The next day I saw Justin as I was pulling into the parking lot before school, and again on my way to Biology. As I left the gym, I literally almost ran into him, which would have been horrible since I was flushed and sweaty from attempting to play badminton without injuring myself or anyone else around me. Luckily, I hadn't—run into Justin, that is—as far as my gym class goes let's just say Coach Reid is just lucky we weren't hitting anything heavier than birdies with those rackets or something other than my dignity (and let's face it, probably my grade) would have been damaged.

I saw Justin again at lunch, though this time he was sitting with Thomas McGregor and the other jocks. It wasn't the Carrie and Brittany table, but it may as well have been. Janie Roberts was there too. Probably still trying to get her claws into him, I thought smugly. Then it occurred to me maybe she already had, and that was why they were sitting together, and for some reason the idea of Justin dating Janie really got under my skin. I hadn't been happy to see the boy of my dreams sitting with Carrie and Brittany, but honestly, I couldn't blame him. I mean, if I were a boy, I'd probably want them too. But Janie? He deserved better.

I saw Justin several more times as I struggled through the rest of my day. In fact, it seemed every time I turned around there he was, and not just at school. I saw him at the library, the grocery store, the gas station. I wasn't sure how I hadn't noticed him before. Justin was everywhere and every day I decided that I should say something to him—anything. Except while I seemed acutely aware of his presence, he seemed completely oblivious to mine. So every time I wanted to approach him I would chicken out.

What if he doesn't remember me? Or worse, he remembers and doesn't care?

In my mind, I could see how our reunion would go. At first, he would be confused and unsure. Then, there would be that moment when his face would light up with dawning recognition, he would be so excited he would hug me, and we would pick up where we left off seven years ago.

That's how I wanted it to go, but what if it didn't. If I never approached him, that image in my mind would remain intact, and I could forever believe that *if* I had approached him he would have been happy to see me. But, if I actually did said hi, and his reaction was different, then I could never go back. Plus, it would not only affect my future but also how I viewed our relationship in the past, and I wasn't certain I was ready to find out that I didn't mean as much to him as he did to me.

So, I decided to hold on to the dream. I watched him from afar, hoping he might notice me, fearing he actually would, and I tried to get on with my life. Until October 5th.

My birthday.

I had been dreading my birthday for half a year, watching it loom ever closer like some impending disaster. It would be my first birthday alone.

The night before the fateful day, I was so upset that I didn't want to go to sleep. Though I was tired, I continued to stay up, finding things to occupy my time as if that might hold it off a little longer. I fell asleep on the couch to muted reruns of the *Andy Griffith Show*.

Pale October sunlight was streaming through the blinds in my living room. I had been having the most beautiful dream. But, as I watched the dust motes floating in the shaft of sunlight under the window, I couldn't recall what the dream was about.

When it was obvious that my dream was gone for good, I sat up and stretched, glancing up at the clock.

8:10!

In a rush, I threw on some fresh clothes, brushed my teeth, and pulled my hair back into a rough ponytail. When I pulled out of my parking space five minutes later, I was thankful that I only lived a few blocks from the school.

I'd always been law abiding when it came to my driving, with the exception of speeding occasionally, but as I approached the intersection of Franklin and Jefferson, I fully intended to just pause at the stop sign. But when I crested the hill, a flat-bedded truck loaded with hay turned onto Jefferson in front of me, and I came to a screeching halt. All the progress I had made with my haste down Franklin Street evaporated as the truck and I took the next block at a snail's pace. I couldn't tell exactly how fast we were going, because the speedometer in my Neon wouldn't gauge anything less than ten miles per hour. But my frustration didn't peak until an old lady and her dog passed me on their morning walk.

Determined to get to school, I swerved blindly to the left to see if I could pass, and was nearly clipped by a little red Metro in the oncoming lane. I cursed loudly, and quickly maneuvered my car away from the yellow line. After that, I resorted to glowering at the back of the truck driver's head while I silently told the man to pull over as if he could really hear me. Then something strange happened. It felt like my head exploded, only in a good way. As if all of those powerful thoughts had built up so much pressure in my head, that they broke free, spilling out like telepathic lava. The air in my car felt charged—static, and then nothing.

I looked around, expecting…something… to have happened, but nothing did, and I exhaled a breath I hadn't known I had been holding. Then the truck in front of me did the strangest thing, it pulled over.

It's just a coincidence, I told myself. But my hands were shaking as I steered around the back of the truck.

He probably just noticed me behind him, and pulled over because he's a nice guy. It has nothing to do with me or whatever just happened. Because nothing happened.

I smiled at my foolishness, and waved my thanks to the driver. But something about the blank look on his face, made me think that he hadn't pulled over simply because he was a nice guy. But that was a crazy thought, and I quickly dismissed it, telling myself I was just on edge because I was late.

Looking back, I think I knew, even then, what had happened. I just wasn't ready to accept it yet.

☐

Had I somehow made him pull over?

No! That was insane. Of course, I hadn't. And the fact that I was even considering the notion that I might have some sort of psychic powers had me thinking I should be reading a little less *Vampire Diaries*, and a little more nonfiction, like my Biology book.

Mr. Pruitt had given the class a worksheet on genetic traits, and I was more than a little lost. I really needed to start paying more attention during his lectures. I knew he'd just told us something about sex-linked traits, but I could not remember what they were. And it didn't help that the tall boy who was sitting next to me kept giving me these weird looks.

I tried to look straight ahead, and pretend he wasn't there, but when someone is staring at you that intensely it's pretty hard not to notice.

I really wish he'd stop doing that, I thought, and to my surprise, he stopped.

That was weird. It was almost like...

My thought was cut short by the bell, and I headed off to the gym with an uneasy feeling in the pit of my stomach. That feeling just got worse when I got to the gym and realized we were playing basketball.

I took my time getting dressed, dreaming up scenarios, while I did so, where Coach Reid would actually let me sit out or make me walk laps or something—anything but make me play. When I finally left the locker room, the rest of my class had already been divided up evenly into teams. Coach Reid caught sight of me, and I braced myself. Ever since the badminton incident I hadn't exactly been his favorite student, and on top of that now I was late. This wasn't going to be pretty. But then the strangest thing happened. The coach looked at his even teams and back at me.

"Loveless, you're late. But since we've already picked teams, why don't you sit this one out?"

All I could do was stare. Was this some kind of birthday present from the universe or had Coach Reid finally caught on to the fact that flying objects and I don't get along so well? And when you get right down to it, that's all P.E. is— a whole class of flying objects.

Whatever his reasons, I wasn't about to object. I quickly and quietly made my way to the bleachers. I kept waiting for him to change his mind, but he didn't.

As strange as his kindness was (if that's what it was), I wasn't really concerned until I noticed the looks he kept

34

giving me. For the rest of the hour Coach Reid kept giving me these looks that were alarmingly similar to the looks my neighbor from biology had been giving me.

That queasy feeling, which had momentarily vanished, was back. Something strange was going on, and unfortunately, that was just the beginning.

In Art, Ms. Rosie gave me an extension on my perspective project, *before* I asked for one. And in Spanish— where I'm always lost because Mr. Cox insists on speaking in Spanish most of time—Mr. Cox taught in English.

I know it sounds crazy, but everything unusual that was happening, seemed to happen right after I thought about it or wished for it, and by lunchtime I was starting to get the feeling that I was somehow making things happen. So, I had this plan to show myself, that it was all in my head and that I just hadn't had enough sleep or something. My imagination had to be getting the better of me and I was going to prove it. All I needed was a guinea pig.

I looked around at the crowded cafeteria, really seeing the people around me for the first time all day. I glanced at Amanda for a moment, before continuing my search. Amanda was a friend (not a close one, but still a friend), and friends don't mess with each other's heads. The next person who came to mind was Justin, but that was too personal. I needed someone I didn't care about.

I scanned the room, and saw a girl I had never seen before getting in line to get a tray. Perfect.

I have no personal feeling for her at all; I don't even know her name.

Now that I had a test subject, I was nervous.

Unsure what I needed to do, I just stared at her, hoping to feel some kind of connection, but it didn't seem to be working.

Maybe I need to tell her to do something.

Drop your tray.

"Winter are you okay?"

"What?" I turned to Amanda who was watching me.

"You've been staring pretty hard at the girl over there. Do you know her or something?"

"No. I was just…trying to figure out if I knew her." It sounded lame, even to me.

"And do you?"

I glanced at the girl and back at Amanda. "No, I guess not."

Then I heard a tray clatter to the floor.

"Poor girl. That would be so embarrassing," Amanda said, watching the girl pick her food off the floor.

Instantly I felt ashamed.

"Do you know her? Is she always that clumsy?" I asked, still holding out hope that I hadn't caused her accident.

"I've never seen her before, she must be new."

I felt about three inches high.

Not only am I a freak who could control people with my mind, but I also pick on unsuspecting new students and humiliate them in the cafeteria. Although, the girl might just be a klutz. Or maybe she has nerve damage that makes her hands unable to grip properly. Or maybe, and more likely, she just tripped. It was a bad experiment.

There were too many variables. I was going to have to try again.

I was going to have to make someone do something they would never do otherwise. To do that I needed someone I knew. Someone I knew and didn't like, so I wouldn't feel bad if it worked. And I knew just the person. Billy Thompson.

Billy Thompson was captain of the football team, and super popular. He was also a self-centered jerk. Back before school had started, at that party I went to, he had hit on me. And apparently, he was not used to rejection, because after that he began calling me a cat lady. (And while I realize that I, in fact, do have a cat. Owning a cat and being a cat lady are two entirely different things.) Luckily the name hadn't stuck.

Billy was the perfect guinea pig, and I knew exactly what I was going make him do. Something he would never do, especially not with everyone watching.

I didn't have to look to find him. I knew where Billy was. He was sitting at the table across the room surrounded by

39

the other athletes and beautiful people. Justin sometimes sat at

that table. Today was one of those days, but I tried not to think

about him. Instead, I focused my attention on the boy three

people to his left. Then closing my eyes, I hurled a command

in his direction.

Chapter 4

"Winter?"

I opened my eyes and peeked up at Billy who was standing over me. I tried to ask him what he wanted, but my mouth had gone dry, and I couldn't seem to find the words. Besides, I knew what he wanted.

"Winter, do you want to go out this weekend?"

I knew it was coming, but that didn't make it any easier. And I felt suddenly nauseous.

It worked. I did it all, the guy in the truck, the boy in Biology, Coach Reid, all of it. Oh no! I made that girl drop her lunch. What's wrong with me? I am *some kind of freak.*

There was no air in the room.

"Winter?" Billy asks again.

I was going to be sick. I could feel the contents of my stomach sitting at the back of my throat, just waiting for my mouth to open so they could escape. So, without a word, I stood up and rushed for the nearest exit. The floor tilted beneath me, and a white haze filled the room, blocking out everything but the door. I needed to reach the door, but my ears were buzzing, and my feet couldn't seem to find the floor. I felt myself falling. Then everything went black.

☐

A sea of faces was staring at me, or something behind me. I really couldn't tell which.

Why are they staring at me like that? And why are they all so tall?

They looked like giants, but I recognized some of them.

That red-haired boy in the back, for example, sits behind me in Algebra, and that boy with the sandy blonde hair has a locker two doors down from mine.

Actually, I recognized all of them.

I must be dreaming.

I wished they would stop staring at me. It was making me uncomfortable. Then I saw one face, closer than the rest, and I smiled.

Justin.

I was glad Justin was in this dream, but I wished he didn't look so lost.

He should be smiling. He always had a great smile.

What's that behind him? That's funny, it almost looks like the ceiling of the cafeteria. But if that's the ceiling, then...

I sat up so quickly the room began to spin, and I grabbed my head.

43

"Winter, can you hear me?"

Justin was so close his breath tickled my skin, and I shivered.

"Look at me."

He didn't have to ask, I couldn't keep my eyes off him. He looked so handsome, with his hair falling in his eyes like that. His eyes were even more beautiful than I remembered. I met his gaze and couldn't seem to look away.

"How long was I out?" I asked in a voice calmer than I felt.

"A couple of minutes."

"I didn't throw up did I?"

Justin smiled for the first time, "No."

"Good."

"Can you stand up?"

44

As I began to get up, he offered his hand to help. The moment we touched, I felt a tingling in my hand as if it had never really been awake until that moment.

Justin took my elbow in his other hand, and the tingling traveled up my arm. My entire forearm was buzzing, as if an electric current was flowing through it. Now that I was on my feet again Justin let go, taking the feeling with him.

I looked around, realizing we still had a group of on-lookers. Billy was among them, and I remembered why I had passed out in the first place. I looked at the door expectantly, the need to escape returning.

"Let's get you out of here," Justin said.

But when we started toward the door, the floor tilted and dizziness overtook me again. Then, just as I was about to fall, I felt a familiar tingling in my lower back, and together Justin and I made our way out the door.

45

"How are you feeling?"

"I'm fine," I said. My voice sounded weak.

"Says the girl who nearly just fainted for a second time."

"Fine, I'm a little dizzy, but it's getting better," I said a little stronger.

With every step, his body brushed against my arm, setting it on fire, making it hard to think. I was so distracted, that it was a few minutes before I even cared where we were going.

"This isn't the way to Mrs. Howitzer's room."

"You aren't going to algebra today," Justin said, and continued to guide me out of the building.

"Then where are we going?"

"To my car," Justin said, glancing over at me, "so I can take you to the doctor."

46

"Why? I'm fine."

"Well, for starters you just passed out, and secondly I'm pretty sure I heard your head hit the floor when you did."

"I'm telling you, I'm fine." But even as I said it, another wave of dizziness hit me and I fell into Justin's side.

"I'd feel a lot better hearing that from a qualified physician could check you out and make sure."

"What about the rest of the day? We didn't even sign out."

"You know you can leave school whenever you want," Justin said, putting me into his car.

When he got in, I asked, "But what about you?"

"I'll be fine."

"So, says the boy who is cutting class."

Justin smiled, and my heart sped up. "Do you pass out every time a boy asks you out?"

"How did you…?"

Justin hesitated, looking away. "It was pretty obvious why Billy went over there."

I blushed and turned to look out my window. "What if I do?"

Justin started the car and I couldn't be sure, but as we pulled out of the parking lot I thought I heard him say, "Then I'll have to remember to catch you."

☐

It was a short drive to the hospital and an even shorter wait in the small emergency room.

"I can't believe you actually took me to the emergency room."

Justin ignored me and asked, "What's your full name?"

"You know I could fill that out."

"What is your full name?" Justin repeated, unrelenting.

"This is ridiculous, just give me the form."

"Fine," he said and began to write, "Winter Marie Loveless."

"What? Marie's not my middle name."

"Since you won't tell me yours I took a gamble. Besides, it's only paper work, at a hospital. I'm sure it doesn't really matter."

"Okay, you want to know my middle name?" I asked.

"I wouldn't have asked if I didn't."

"It's Sky," I mumbled.

Justin looked at me and kind of smiled. "I didn't you're your middle name was Sky. Winter Sky Loveless. That's nice," he said without a hint of mockery.

"Didn't you ever wonder why I didn't just go by my middle name instead of Winter?"

49

"Not really. I always liked your name."

"Yeah, well you didn't grow up with it."

Our eyes met for a second before Justin looked back down at the form on the clipboard.

"Address?"

"2512 Ranch Motel Drive Seriously, I could fill that out. My arms are fine."

"No, I've got it. Phone number?"

"Just hand me the form. I'll have it done it like two seconds."

"As you wish."

I rolled my eyes at the movie reference, and began filling in my phone number and insurance information.

"So, what is your number?"

Startled, I looked over at Justin sitting beside the bed in my cubicle. Then I did something I'd never done before. I grabbed his hand and wrote my number on it. I wasn't sure what I expected to happen, but after a few seconds of awkward silence, I turned away and gave the form on my lap way more attention than was actually necessary. Maybe there was something wrong with my brain after all.

"You didn't even know my middle name. What were you going to do when you got down to my family history?"

"Ask a lot of questions."

The curtain separating my bed from the rest of the ER was pulled back, and a middle-aged man with a gut and a clipboard entered.

"Hi, I'm Dr. Matson. What seems to be the problem today?"

I handed Dr. Matson my paperwork, and he began looking through it.

"Winter fainted at lunch, and hit her head pretty hard on the floor when she fell. I was afraid she might have a concussion, so I've been trying to keep her alert and talking."

Keeping me talking? He was only talking to me because he thought I had a concussion? Mortified I glanced at my phone number written on his hand

Dr. Matson pulled out a penlight and began shining it in my eyes.

"Follow the light with your eyes. Good. Now look up. Perfect."

When he'd finished looking at my eyes, he put away the light and began to feel my head with his hands. Then he grabbed my wrist and began timing my heart rate.

"Winter, is this the first time you've fainted?"

"Yes. I think I just got up too fast."

"Any dizziness or headache now?"

"No."

His hands moved to my neck, feeling my lymph nodes, before he let go and picked up my chart.

"Winter, your blood work came back normal, your blood pressure looks good, and you don't seem to have a concussion. But we can't know for sure without a CT scan. If you wish to have one, I'll order it, but in my opinion you don't need it."

"That's okay. So, am I good to go?"

"Yes," he said, writing on my chart. "If you have any more dizziness or develop a headache, blurred vision, or have any trouble moving or speaking in the next 48 hours let me know."

"Okay."

I took the discharge paperwork he handed me, and he left.

"Are you satisfied?" I asked Justin.

"Yes."

"Now will you please leave and close the curtain behind you so I can get dressed?"

Chapter 5

I leaned my head against the headrest of Justin's car, and closed my eyes. I needed a minute to myself. This was turning out to be the worst birthday ever. I just hoped Justin wasn't tired of having me around already, because between my new *talent* and passing out, he'd been the only good thing that'd happened, and I really didn't want to be alone at the moment.

I opened my eyes and watched the downtown shops go by, enjoying the silence. When we turned onto Pershing Street, I finally asked where we were going.

"To my house," Justin said.

When we pulled up to the detached garage, I turned to him and smiled.

"I remember this place. You live here?"

"Yeah. You didn't know that?"

"I didn't even know you lived in Salem until I saw you at school." I stepped out of the car and looked at the house where I first met Justin.

"You spent the whole summer here. How didn't you know where we lived?" Justin asked, sounding truly amused.

"I was five. I didn't know where I was. And besides, your family vacationed at a different place every year. For all I knew this was just another vacation home."

I followed Justin inside and was surprised by how familiar it all still was. While Justin looked through the mail, I went down the hall to his room and opened the door.

"Sure, you can go into my room," Justin said, coming up behind me.

"Technically it was my room too." I entered and sat on the bed, and Justin followed. "Once upon a time."

"So, what do you think?"

"It's smaller than I remember but just as messy." I bumped his shoulder playfully, causing a tingling sensation that reminded me that we weren't five anymore, and suddenly I felt self-conscious sitting on his bed.

"Yeah, well I haven't had you around to clean up after me."

"Well, don't get your hopes up. I'm not cleaning your room."

"In that case, c'mon. I've got something to show you."

Justin led me back to the front of the house and into the living room, where their old console TV had been replaced with a flat panel TV that covered the large space above the fireplace.

"Nice," I said. "It sure beats my little thirteen inch."

"Want to watch a movie?"

"Sure. What have you got?"

"You'll see."

Justin put in a DVD, turned down the lights, and sat next to me on the leather sofa. When the DVD menu came on, I turned to Justin astonished.

"Milo and Otis?"

"I know it's probably not your favorite anymore, but I thought it might be fun to watch. But if you'd rather watch something else we can."

"No, this is perfect. I just can't believe you remembered."

Justin looked at me. "Some things you never forget."

Looking at him in the dim light, sitting so close, I felt the urge to kiss him again, but my will power was stronger this time. "It was your fault it was my favorite, you know."

"Why's that?"

58

"Milo and Otis are such good friends that even though they separate and have their own adventures, they remain friends forever and eventually find each other again. It kind of reminded me of us," I said shyly, embarrassed by my confession.

Maybe I am suffering some kind of head injury.

I could feel Justin watching me, but I stared hard at the screen, afraid to meet his eyes, and after a long silence he said, "Winter, I'll always be your friend."

I smiled warmly at him.

"Are you hungry?"

I nodded and Justin said he'd be right back. When he returned, he had a plate of cupcakes in his hand. They were chocolate with Halloween orange icing, and one of them had a lit candle in it.

"I know it's not much but, Happy Birthday."

"How did you…?"

"Like I said, some things you never forget. Make a wish."

I watched the flame dance as I contemplated my wish. I hadn't forgotten how powerful my thoughts could be, and I was almost giddy with anticipation as I wished for what I wanted most in the world, and blew out the candle.

I wish I had my mom back.

Chapter 6

That Sunday, like every other Sunday, I visited my mom. I hated how fragile she looked laying there with so many wires and tubes hooked up to her, but I tried to act as normal as possible. If it was true she could hear me, I didn't want her know how scared I was.

I was telling my mom all about Justin, when I heard a gasp. Turning, I saw a woman standing in the doorway. Her brown hair was streaked with gray, but her skin was smooth and seemed to glow from within. She was beautiful in an unsettling sort of way, and vaguely familiar.

"Are you here to visit my mom? If so, I'll be done in a few minutes," I said, trying to ignore the strange way she was looking at me.

"You're Paige's daughter. I should have known, you look just like her," she said, stepping into the room. "except for your eyes."

"They're my father's. Do I know you?"

"No," she said, "but I knew your mother a long time ago."

I just watched her cautiously, waiting for her to continue.

"I'm Doris Asher," she said as if I should know her name and extended her hand.

"I'm Winter," I said, not taking her hand. Eventually she dropped it.

"I knew you were one of us when I saw you the other day. I just didn't realize who you were."

"You were walking your dog," I said, finally realizing where I'd seen her before.

"Yes, and you were very angry," Doris said.

"What do you mean 'one of us'?" I didn't like the way this conversation was going.

Doris opened her mouth to say something and stopped, letting her gaze really take me in. "You don't know, do you?"

I took a cautious step back, backing into the side of my mom's bed. "Know what?"

"Who you are. What you are." Doris stopped, searching my face for any recognition of what she was talking about, before continuing in a hushed voice. "You're a Siren."

"I'm sorry, a what?"

"I can help you," Doris said and took a piece of paper and a pen from her purse. "Here is my number. Call me anytime."

Doris laid the paper on a table by my mom's bed, and when I reached for the nurse call button said, "Don't worry

I'm leaving. A word of caution though, be careful, you're more powerful than you think."

Doris gave my mom a final glance and with one last look at my eyes, she turned and left the room.

I let out the breath I'd been holding, and sat down like a deflated balloon. What had that been about? A Siren? The woman was clearly disturbed.

Shaken and upset I reached for my mom's hand, and wished for the thousandth time that she would wake up and make everything better.

Chapter 7

The phone was ringing when I got in the door, and I rushed to get it.

"Hello?"

"Hey, did I wake you up?"

Justin. My heart fluttered, but I tried to sound casual.

"No, I just got in, actually," I said, closing the door I'd left open in my hurry to get to the phone.

"Really? I just got up." Justin sounded sleepy.

I checked the clock. "Justin, it's almost eleven!"

"I know. So, did you just get back from church or something?"

"No, I was visiting my mom."

Justin was quiet for a second. "How did that go?"

"Weird, actually."

"Do you want to talk about it?"

"Not really." Just thinking about the conversation with Doris sent a shiver down my spine.

"If you change your mind, I'm always here to listen."

"I'll keep that in mind, but right now I'd rather just think about something else."

"Well, in that case," Justin paused, "would you like to have dinner with me tonight?"

I dropped the phone.

Was Justin asking me out?

I had been trying so hard to hide my romantic feelings; it hadn't occurred to me that he might want to be more than just friends. Why would he? I quickly picked up the phone.

"I'm sorry, what?" I asked, trying to sound calm.

"I was wondering if you would like to have dinner tonight. My mom would be there too. She's really been wanting to see you again."

I felt like an idiot. Dinner with his family. Not a date.

"Of course, what time?"

"Probably seven."

"Yeah, that would be nice." Now that my heart was back to normal, it did sound nice.

"Great, I'll pick you up at 6:30."

I started to protest, to say I could drive myself, when I realized he was already off the line. Bewildered I hung up the phone.

"Looks like you'll be eating alone tonight, Boris," I said to the white cat sleeping in the square of sunlight below the window.

Boris shifted his position but kept sleeping. He
wouldn't miss me.

My stomach growled, and I remembered that, as usual,
I hadn't eaten breakfast before visiting my mom. I searched
through my cupboards, and poured myself a bowl of Cocoa
Pebbles. I would need to go grocery shopping later.

*What did she mean I'm a siren? What's a siren? Did
she mean a siren, as in the mythological creature that tried to
kill Odysseus? It didn't matter, she was just a nut job, and
yet...*

I decided I would look the word 'siren' up online.
Doris may be a crazy person, but it wouldn't hurt to look it up.
Maybe there was another definition I'd never heard of, like:
girl who had never had a boyfriend who happens to own a cat.
But I doubted it.

When the internet finally connected (all I had was dial up), I typed in siren and hit search. There were hundreds of hits, several of which were about sirens of the silver screen. I quickly ruled them out, as well as those pertaining to emergency vehicles. I really doubted that was what Doris had in mind. I decided to look up the definition of the word.

1. Any of a group of female and partly human creatures in Greek mythology that lured mariners to destruction by their singing. 2. A woman who sings with enchanting sweetness; temptress.

So much for that idea.

I turned off the computer. I didn't need to read any more. Doris was clearly bonkers, unless she thought I was some kind of femme fatale, in which case she was still bonkers because that would imply that boys not only noticed me but also desired me.

This was ridiculous. I had five hours to kill before I got to see Justin again (yes I counted), and I was not going to spend the whole time dissecting what some crazy old chick had said to me. I had homework to do, groceries to buy.

Plenty of things to occupy my time.

☐

With ten minutes until Justin was supposed to pick me up, I checked my reflection for the millionth time. I didn't know why I was so nervous. Justin and I had been spending most of our free time together for nearly a week now.

We are friends. It's not a date.

But that didn't mean that I couldn't try to look my best, did it?

I was wearing my favorite navy blue knit blouse because it compliments my complexion and my skinny jeans because they make me look like I have curves. My hair was down and was being kinder to me than usual, which is good because I suck when it comes to styling it. I'd also picked up some makeup at the store.

Even I had to admit that I looked good, and I returned to the living room to wait for Justin.

At 6:28, Justin arrived at my door smelling like aftershave and holding a single pink rose. He was wearing relaxed fit jeans and a black sweater that contrasted with his pale skin, making his dark eyes, which were watching me, seem even more intense.

"This is for you." Justin handed me the rose.

"Thank you. Let me quickly put this in some water then we can leave."

I took the rose and headed into my kitchenette to find a vase, all the while trying to process what the rose meant.

Roses would usually imply romantic feelings, but it was pink. I knew yellow meant friendship, but I had no idea what pink meant.

I placed the vase on the table, and followed Justin out to his car where he opened the door for me.

"You look nice, by the way," Justin said, glancing at me out of the corner of his eye, as he backed the car out onto the road.

"Thank you. You don't look too bad yourself," I said, trying desperately to decipher the mixed signals Justin was sending me.

"You know I do have a car. I could have driven myself," I said.

"This way I get to spend more time with you." Justin reached over and squeezed my hand sending the now familiar electrifying sensation coursing through my hand and up my arm.

"Okay, it's your gas," I said trying to sound as though my heart wasn't racing.

"Yep. So, how was the rest of your day?" Justin said casually, letting go of my hand.

"You mean after I talked to you? I did homework and went grocery shopping. *Real* exciting, I know. How about your day? You do anything after you *woke up*?"

"Oh, you know, the usual. I stole a car, won the Super Bowl, and rounded off the day by saving the world. Typical stuff." Justin gave me a cocky smile.

"Nothing too exciting for you either, huh?"

"I played playstation," Justin admitted.

"All day?"

"Most of it."

"Aren't you on the football team or something?"

"Yeah, and basketball."

"I thought you guys were supposed to be active and crap."

"It's a common misconception."

We arrived at his house, and my former awkwardness returned.

What does his mom think this is? Is this just another dinner with his family, or is this one of those dinners where his mom gets to check out his new...whatever I was to him?

On the porch, Justin stopped me. "What's wrong?"

"What do you mean?"

"You only chew your lip like that when you're nervous."

Though his face was in shadow, I could see he was smiling. Suddenly, all of my angst went away, and it was just

74

Justin and me like it had been all week, like we'd been for years. Because when I stopped obsessing over my romantic feelings, being with Justin was like being home.

It was like breathing.

Then he took my hand in his, leading me through the door, and the tightness in my stomach returned.

□

Dinner was tacos. Any misconceptions I had about whether it was some kind of date ended when I saw the fast food bags on the table. That pretty much solidified me as just part of his family. He was not interested in me.

I was like a sister to him, but the way I felt about him is far from sisterly.

Even though we were eating fast food, his mom still set the table as if it were a home cooked meal. Then Justin surprised me by pulling out my chair for me.

What was that about?

"I'm so glad you could join us for dinner," Mrs. Smith said, offering me the sour cream.

"Thank you for having me."

"It's no problem. It doesn't seem right for you to have to be alone so much. If Brad were here, he'd be happy to see you again too," Mrs. Smith said.

Though her words were kind, they made me uncomfortable. Justin had told me that his dad had died, but I didn't like to think about it. Mr. Smith had always been so full of life. He was the one who used to cheer me up whenever Justin had made me cry. He taught me how to burp and how to swim. He was the only real father figure I ever had. I didn't like talking about him any more than I liked talking about my mother.

"So, your mother is at the nursing home over on Highway 72? I'll have to go and visit her some time," Mrs. Smith continued.

"I'm sure she would like that," I said, wishing we could talk about something else.

"So, I totally bombed the world history test I had on Friday," Justin said catching my eye.

Thank you, I telegraphed to him, and then I stopped, catching my breath.

Justin didn't seem to have noticed anything, and I relaxed a little. I needed to be more careful. The last person I needed or wanted to know about my freakishness was Justin.

"What? You said you studied for that," Mrs. Smith said, taking the bait.

I knew for a fact that Justin had studied for that test. We wouldn't know our score until Tuesday, but I really doubted he had done badly. Because the truth was that he had helped *me* study for that test.

"I did study. I'm just saying I don't think I did too well," Justin said with a mouth full of taco.

He was laying it on thick, and it was working.

"Justin, you know better than to talk with food in your mouth," his mom said.

Justin just nudged my leg under the table, and winked at me when his mom wasn't looking. He was just being friendly but it gave me butterflies just the same. When Mrs. Smith felt she had thoroughly reprimanded Justin, she turned her attention back to me.

"Winter, are you going to the Harvest Ball, next weekend?" Mrs. Smith asked, when we had finished off the box of tacos.

The Harvest Ball was the first formal dance of the year. STUCO had put up flyers advertising it the previous week, but truthfully, I'd had more important things on my mind and hadn't paid them much attention.

"Well, nobody has asked me yet, so probably not," I said daring to glance up at Justin when I did.

"You should still go. It sounds like fun. Justin, who is it you're taking?"

"Janie Roberts," Justin said quietly, avoiding my eyes.

I reached for my glass, knocking it over, spilling water all over the table.

"Oh, I'm sorry, Mrs. Smith. I'll get a towel and clean it up." Cheeks burning, I rushed into the kitchen.

"The towels are under the sink," Mrs. Smith said, coming in behind me.

"Thanks." I leaned down to look under the sink.

"Winter, I know what you're doing."

"I thought you said they were down here."

"Not about the towel. I know what you're doing to my son, and I want you to stop."

A chill crept down my back. "I don't know what you are talking about."

"Winter, I know what you're, and I see the way he looks at you."

"Mrs. Smith, Justin and I are just friends, nothing more."

"If you really care about Justin the way I think you do, you'll keep it that way. Just remember that it's not real."

Confused and more than a little hurt, I grabbed a towel and left the kitchen. I thought Justin's mom had always liked me.

I guess I was good enough to be his friend, but not good enough to be anything more.

Her comment, about knowing what I was, reminded me a little too much of the conversation I'd had with Doris.

I sopped up the mess, thankful I was only drinking water, and sat back down feeling queasy. Justin was watching me, but I couldn't bring myself to look at him. I wished I'd brought my own car.

"Justin, it's getting late. I think it's time you took Winter home," Mrs. Smith said from the kitchen door.

"Sure," Justin said, still watching me. "Come on, Winter. I'll get your coat."

Outside, the cold night air settled my stomach a little, though I didn't think I could get any more embarrassed at this point, even if I threw up.

We drove to my apartment in silence, and I was surprised when Justin got out and walked me to my door.

Why does he insist on prolonging my humiliation?

I started to unlock my door without saying anything.

"Winter, wait," Justin said, grabbing my hand, sending an electric current through it. Only this time it made me want to cry, and I was glad my porch light wasn't on.

"What?"

"I'm sorry. About Janie." Justin was still holding my hand, and stepped closer.

I looked down, because even in shadow, Justin was standing close enough to see my tears if I looked at him.

"You don't have to explain anything to me. We're just friends."

"Are we?" Justin's voice was husky, and I couldn't help but look up at him.

His fingers were still twined with mine, and when I met his eyes, the bottom of my stomach dropped out. He was standing close, and I swear it felt like every fiber of my body was trying to pull me closer, trying to close the short distance between us. Justin reached for my face with his other hand, caressing my cheek and brushing the tears away with his thumb, leaving a trail of fire in its wake. I couldn't breathe. I couldn't speak.

"She asked me, before...before this. If I'd known..."

"It's okay," I stammered nervously.

"I don't want you to be alone. I'll save you a dance if you come."

83

What does that mean?

"Don't worry about it. I probably won't even go."

Justin's gaze lingered on me a moment longer than necessary.

"Goodnight, Winter," Justin said, stepping back off my door step. Just before he let go of my hand he brought it to his lips, sending a trail of fire blazing straight to my heart. Then he was getting into his car, leaving the air around me feeling cold and vacant.

I leaned against my door and watched him drive away, afraid that if I moved, my quivering legs wouldn't support me, and I'd had about as much embarrassment as I could handle for one night.

When Justin's Blazer was out of sight, I turned and stumbled into my apartment. Once inside I stopped and touched the place on my hand where Justin's lips had been, and closed my eyes remembering the pleasant tingling flame that had ignited under my skin. When I started imagining how his lips would feel on mine I stopped myself.

We're just friends, I think.

I wanted nothing more than to curl up on my bed, and let my subconscious mind deal with my problems for a while, but there was one thing I had to do first.

I went to my closet, and pulled out a box I'd stored in the back behind my shoes. When I had packed my life away to move here, I had labeled each box with a magic marker, but I didn't need to read the list scrawled on the side to know what was in it.

When it had been clear my mom wasn't going to wake up anytime soon, I had sold our furniture, and boxed up her other personal items, which hadn't been very much. When you moved around as much as we had, you learned not to hold onto things. I'd taken my mother's clothes to the nursing

85

home, so she wouldn't have too wear those hospital gowns she hated, and the rest of her personal affects I'd packed into this box.

I settled myself on my bedroom floor, and gingerly opened the box. On top was an old yearbook, and under that a photo album from the same time period. I put these aside and began digging through baby memorabilia and loose greeting cards that my mother had saved for whatever reason. It was painful to search through. Each item flooded my mind with memories of my mother and the life we had had before, and soon tears were streaming down my cheeks but I kept searching for what I was looking for—my mom's diary.

I found it in the bottom corner of the box next to the necklace she had been wearing when the accident had happened. I pulled them both out.

I laid the necklace aside and examined the diary. It was bound in black fabric, with a lavender ribbon marking a page somewhere in the middle. If my mom knew anything about what was happening to me, or the strange accusations from Doris or Mrs. Smith, it would be in this book.

But is it right to read my mom's most personal thoughts?

I laid the book and necklace on the bed, and packed the rest of the stuff back into the box and put it away. I picked up the necklace and looked at it. It looked ancient, with a sturdy gold chain, and a large ruby pendant. For the longest time, I hadn't even been able to look at this necklace. It was the only thing that had been pulled from the car that hadn't been damaged. But holding it now, it felt like my mother was closer to me somehow. I started to put it on, but changed my mind and put it in my pocket instead.

87

Then I picked up the book. And opened it to the marked page.

Winter sang to me today, and I knew what I'd feared was true. That ritual Ellie and I did must not have worked. She had tried to tell me, but I hadn't listened. I knew she never got the voice, but mine was gone too, so I thought she was wrong. If she hadn't gotten the gift, then where had it gone? It must have been with me the whole time, because Winter is living proof. There is no doubt in my mind that she is a Siren. I have to find a way to suppress it. Her father cannot ever find out...

I closed the book, and sat on the bed cradling my head in my hands. I didn't need to read anymore. Doris had called me one of *them*, a Siren. Mrs. Smith had said she knew what I was. Her first name is Eleanor, but she must have gone by Ellie back then. My mom had confided in her, even done some ritual.

What am I?

I curled into the fetal position on my bed and cried.

Mom, I need you. Why couldn't you have explained this to me? I don't know what to think anymore.

Though I felt like I was losing my mind, one thing was certain. It was time to call Doris and find out what she had to say.

Chapter 8

I called Doris early the next morning, and she told me
to come right over. She only lived a block away, so within
minutes she was opening her door and letting me in.

Doris's bracelets jingled when she walked and her
floral skirt billowed behind her as she led me through the
entryway to a dimly lit living room. It was just getting light
outside, but what little sunlight there was, was blocked out by
the thick drapes that covered the windows. The only light
came from a lamp in the corner that had a red shawl draped
over it.

The room was full of an odd assortment of clutter.
Paintings of Greek goddesses hung on the wall next to dream
catchers and star charts. A chipped ceramic mortar and pestle
sat on a stack of black leather-bound books. A marble bust of

Cleopatra stood in the corner next to a revolutionary musket, and a bearskin rug lay on the floor in front of a colonial, claw footed couch. The only thing tying it all together was age. Everything looked ancient.

I sat gingerly on the couch, and Doris said she would be right back.

I couldn't sit still, and soon I was pacing. As I walked, I absentmindedly handled the little knick knacks and priceless antiques that covered every square inch of the room. I had just set down a large red crystal that was acting as a bookend, when a picture on the next shelf up caught my eye. Staring back at me, from inside the little silver picture frame, was my mother. She was younger, but it was definitely her. She looked like she'd been caught off guard by whoever had taken the picture, and sitting beside her in the picture was Doris.

So, she really did know my mom.

A few minutes later Doris returned, carrying a tray of lemonade. She set it down on the coffee table before sitting down next to me.

"So, tell me, what is your gift?" Doris said eagerly.

"I don't know what you mean."

"What can you do?"

"Mind control," I said.

"Really?" Doris asked, studying me. "Interesting. Will you try it on me?"

"I'm not sure…"

"Just try," Doris looked at me kindly. "Please?"

"Okay."

I looked around the room for an idea of what I could make Doris do.

"Can I request something?" Doris asked, breaking into my thoughts.

My palms felt slick and suddenly I wasn't sure I had ever done anything.

What if I imagined all of it?

"Sure."

"Why don't you try to make me open the drapes?"

"The drapes?" I asked stupidly, turning to look at the heavy curtains covering the window across the room.

"Yes, that way it's a controlled experiment."

"Okay."

Doris relaxed in her winged backed chair and closed her eyes. "I'm ready."

I'd never felt more on the spot, or less sure of myself. The sun had come up behind the maroon curtains, filling the room with a warm glow that made it feel more like sunset than sunrise. I felt suspended in time, and a shiver of anticipation ran through me. This had to work. Determined, I stared hard at

Doris's face, and imagined my thoughts blowing through her mind like an enticing breeze.

Doris, open the drapes.

I watched her face, waiting. After a moment, she opened her eyes and gazed at me, expectantly. And like that, all of my excitement and anticipation crashed down inside of me. It hadn't worked. I was normal after all. And while I knew I should have been relieved, I could feel the disappointment of it burning in my eyes, threatening to spill over, and I stood up and headed for the door.

"I'm sorry, I thought…Well, I don't know what I thought."

As I reached the door, Doris seemed to find her voice. "Wait! What are you talking about? That was incredible."

Incredulously, I stopped with my hand on the doorknob. "I don't know what you just witnessed, but I didn't do anything."

"I haven't been entirely forthright with you. Please, sit back down and let me explain."

I dropped my hand and turned to face Doris, but stayed by the door.

"No, I didn't open the drapes, but I didn't expect to."

I felt my face flush, and I turned to leave again.

"But only because your energy is blocked."

That stopped me.

"What?"

"Please sit down."

I sat.

"Sirens are very powerful, and some of us are gifted. I was gifted with enhanced sight. I can see people's energy, their élan vital."

"Like an aura or something?"

"It's hard to explain. I don't see psychedelic colors or anything. It's more like a light bulb." Doris looked at me, searching for a reaction, but when I said nothing she continued. "It's like every person has a light bulb inside of them. Everyone has this inner glow, which I can only describe as their life force. It's what the Chinese call a person's chi. The more energy they have, the brighter the glow. The majority of people are roughly seventy-five watters, though I've seen my fair share of forty and one hundred-watt people. And then there is us."

"And what do Sirens look like?" I asked, not yet ready to throw myself into that group.

"We are brighter than any light bulb," Doris said, smiling at me. "We shine like the sun, brighter than the sun actually, and whiter. You know how white light is made up of all the colors of the rainbow blended together? Well, I have a feeling that if the light coming off us were broken down into a spectrum it would contain colors yet to be discovered. The energy coming from within us is the purest energy I've ever seen."

"But you said mine is blocked?"

"Yes," Doris said, a quizzical expression crossing her face. "I believe it is this extraordinary energy within each Siren that gives us our abilities. With yours plugged up the way it is, I'd be surprised if you could have a basic déjà vu, the very lowest of psychic abilities, much less practice mind control, but just now even with the blockage I felt it. It wasn't strong enough to make me obey, but I did feel an urge to open the drapes. You say you've actually controlled people?"

"It only happened a couple of times on my birthday, but since then I haven't been able to."

"Your seventeenth birthday?"

"Yeah, how did you know?"

"Lucky guess."

Doris walked a slow circle around me, prodding and examining different areas until she was standing before me again.

"Was that the day you first saw me? Your birthday? The day you discovered your talent?"

"Yeah, it was."

"Amazing, unless…Have you done anything to yourself since then, that could have plugged you up like this?" Doris asked.

"I don't know, since I have no idea what would or wouldn't block my energy."

"Have you used any hallucinogens or methamphetamines?"

"No, and I haven't smoked, or drank, or gotten high on anything else either. I try to avoid drugs, legal or otherwise."

"And I assume you haven't done any rituals that would have depleted your energy."

"Considering that I still don't even know what a siren is, I can assure you that I haven't performed any rituals of any kind."

"Don't be so sure," Doris muttered under her breath before continuing, "I have a theory. What *was* your mom like?"

"My mother *is* a wonderful person," I said, trying to hide the agitation in my voice. "Besides, you knew her. Didn't you?"

"Of course, but that was so long ago. Plus, in her condition, I assume her personality is quite dull at the moment. I was merely wondering what she used to be like."

My agitation quickly turned to anger, but I fought to control it, telling myself Doris hadn't meant to be so uncouth. "She was lively and fun and smart. Why?"

"Did she beat you? Her boyfriends molest you?" Doris asked casually, sitting back down.

I could feel my anger boiling just under the surface. "Just what is your theory?"

"You don't deny it?"

"I didn't feel like dignifying your questions with a response. I've already told you she is great. She is the best mom I could have asked for."

"Don't you mean *was*?" Doris asked with a cruel smirk.

I stopped even trying to control my anger as I hurled the full brunt of it at Doris, *"Don't talk about my mother like that!"*

To my surprise and annoyance, Doris neither cowered nor looked upset in any way. In fact, she smiled warmly up at me. "Tell me to open the drapes again."

"What?"

"Just do it, please."

Fine. *Open the drapes!*

To my utter amazement, her face went blank and she did. Suddenly my knees felt weak.

101

"What did you do to me? How did you...?"

"You were angry with the car in front of you on your birthday, weren't you?"

"Yes, but…"

"My theory is that the blockage isn't new, but the ability to get through it is."

Confused I just stared at her.

"Why don't you come sit back down and I'll apologize and explain."

I sat.

"I am sorry about what I said about your mom, but I needed to make you angry to test my theory. When you got angry last week, as well as just a few moments ago, it created so much pressure within you that you quite literally blew your top. The extra pressure unplugged your temporal chakra, much like a volcano."

102

"My what?"

"Right here." Doris reached over and touched the middle of my forehead.

"But I'm not blocked anymore?" I touched my forehead, expecting it to feel different but it didn't.

"For the time being, no. Your energy is flowing freely, at least through that chakra. So were you to try to influence anyone today it would probably work. But my guess is by tomorrow all of your energy channels will be plugged again."

"But how did the blockage get there?"

"Did your mother ever do any rituals with you?"

"Not that I know of."

"No, she probably would have disguised them as something else. Did she often use holistic drugs, aromatherapy, anything like that?"

103

The passage from my mom's diary flashed through my mind.

I have to find a way to suppress it.

I thought back through the years I had spent traveling the country with my mother. The yoga, the aromatherapy, the sachets, the crystals, the health food. Mom had gone through so many trends I'd lost count.

Had she really just been looking for a way to suppress my energy?

"Yes, we did a lot of different things like that together," I said.

"I think your mom found a way to plug you up, and essentially make you normal." Doris couldn't hide the amazement or the hint of disgust in her voice, as if normal was the worst possible thing to be.

104

"Just how far from normal will I be without the blockage?" I asked, a little nervous.

"Winter, I think it's time I tell you who you are."

Chapter 9

"I'm sure you've heard of Sirens, those mythological creatures whose beautiful voices would lure sailors to their deaths?"

"Yeah, Homer, English II," I murmured.

"Homer wasn't very fond of our kind, but then most people aren't, and haven't been for centuries. You won't find the true story of the Sirens in any book, but our history has been handed down from one generation to the next, from mother to daughter, grandmother to granddaughter all the way back to the Great Flood where our story begins.

Everyone knows the story of Noah and the Ark—how he saved the animals and his family from the greatest natural disaster that has ever occurred—while the rest of the Earth's population was annihilated. But what most people don't realize is that Noah and his family weren't the only ones that survived.

In the days of Noah there lived a descendant of Cain by the name of Lamech. When word of Noah's predictions made their way to the land of Nod, where Lamech lived he believed Noah's words and immediately set out to find Noah and hear what he had to say.

Well, you can imagine what Noah told him. Noah told him that the only way he could survive was to repent of his wicked ways. But Lamech decided to build a boat of his own instead.

But there were problems with his plan from the very beginning. First of all, the only one with any knowledge of boats or how to build them was Noah, and he wasn't exactly offering courses. So, Lamech decided to watch Noah, and copy him on a smaller scale. Then there was the trouble of finding materials. Noah had harvested all the available wood in the area, so Lamech had to travel a great distance to get the wood he needed for construction. Eventually he had collected enough materials, but the night before he planned to begin construction all of his wood caught fire and was destroyed.

Convinced Noah was behind the fire, Lamech confronted him. But Noah denied have done anything, and told Lamech that the fire was a judgment from God.

Lamech refused to give up, and started harvesting more wood, but when the forest where he was cutting his trees caught fire and burned to the ground he finally believed it might be some kind of judgment against him. Instead of listening to Noah's counsel, Lamech became more determined then ever to survive the flood and so made a deal with the devil. Noah had prophesied that all life that breathed air would die—so in exchange for the power to breathe under water Lamech gave up his own soul.

The flood came but Lamech wasn't satisfied with just surviving. He wanted more. So, while everyone around him was fighting against the inevitable, he watched waiting for his opportunity to arrive.

Many children died when the world was flooded, and even in a world so wicked it had to be destroyed God loved the little children. So, he sent his angels to collect their souls and shepherd them to heaven.

Anna was one such angel. She had been told to keep her distance; to call to the children from high above the water, but she couldn't bear to see their fear and confusion as they searched for her, so she swooped down, drawing close enough that the tips of her wings actually brushed the water. And as she caressed the face of an infant floating in the water,

Lamech captured her and dragged her down to his underwater lair, where he kept her until her death.

By death, I mean until she was no more. Angels don't really die. When they are touched by evil, when they are corrupted their souls shatter, but I digress.

Before she died, she bore Lamech fifty children, all of which were girls. History would call them the mermaids. And we are their descendants today.

Now they didn't really have fins or a tail, but they could breathe under water, and because of who their parents where and how they came to be they also had some other special abilities, some of which you already know.

They were beautiful beyond compare and had the voices of angels, and some were gifted with other powers. Eventually, they all left the water, and as you can imagine everywhere they went, people took notice. Some were

110

worshiped as gods, as was the case for Aphrodite, while others were burned as heretics or witches. The mermaids or their daughters the Sirens can be found throughout history: Cleopatra, Helen of Troy, you get the idea. But no matter where they went or with whom they had children one thing was the same. Whenever their daughters reached the age of seventeen they inherited their mother's powers and gifts. So, the powers you have, have been passed from generation to generation until they came to you.

"So, what happens now, since my power is blocked? What will happen to me?"

"You could live out your life being relatively normal, or you could let me unblock your energy and become what you really are."

The way Doris said normal made it sound like a swear word, something extremely undesirable, but I wasn't convinced. Normal was what I'd wanted for most of my life.

"What exactly would happen if you did?"

"Each of your chakras is like a blocked artery right now. The energy isn't going to the places it needs to in order for you to really develop into a mature siren. Once I remove the blockage, the free-flowing chi will produce many changes in you. First of all, you will begin producing a pheromone, quite specific to Sirens. It will make you highly attractive to men. Secondly, your hormone levels will change, kind of like puberty only kinder. Your unusual hormone levels will help to produce physical transformations such as flawless skin, lustrous hair, shapelier body, better teeth, even fuller thicker eyelashes. Basically, we are everything that the cosmetic world wishes to achieve. Third, the energy will also affect

112

your voice. When a Siren sings, she unlocks the full strength of the power within her into whatever capacity she directs her voice. Meaning, whatever your goal is in singing, you can make happen within the confines of the power you possess. The more powerful you are the more you can do."

"Really? Like what kinds of things?"

"While singing, most Sirens have the ability to affect others' emotions, maybe even convince them to do something or act a certain way. But there are some powerful enough to move inanimate objects or even change the weather. It's rare but I've heard of it."

"Like telekinesis?"

"I can see why you might think that, but no. A person with telekinesis can reach out with their mind to push or pull objects like they would with their hands. When a Siren sings it's almost as if she commands the object to move and it obeys of its own accord. But that brings me to the final change—your gift. Once your chi is moving as it should, you will be able to use your gift without any trouble. Not all Sirens are Gifted, not many are. The fact that you are Gifted at all tells me you are special; your vital energy is strong even if I can't see all of it. But I can fix that for you if you allow me."

I was stunned into silence, not really sure what I should do, when I was saved by the bell—literally. All around us, her collection of grandfather clocks began to chime. It was eight o'clock.

"I have to get to class. Do you mind if I think about it?"

"I should warn you that keeping that kind of energy bottled up may not be safe to you or those around you. It's liable to come out sooner or later."

I told her I'd think about it and headed for the door.

114

Chapter 10

So, I can stay like I am, if I want. Would that be so bad?

It was lunchtime and I had been mulling the idea over all day. I had to admit the physical beauty sounded appealing. But did I want to be able to get into people's minds? That still felt wrong to me.

Mom didn't want this life for me, that was obvious, but I was old enough to make my own decision now. The question was whether I wanted this life. As tempting as it sounded, honestly all I wanted was to be normal, to fit in, and being even more different was not going to help. I wanted to forget all about it and go on with my life as though nothing was happening to me, but deep down inside I knew it wouldn't be that easy. Part of me wondered if I really had a choice at all.

Justin had tried to catch me in between classes a couple of times, but I hadn't been ready to talk to him, so I'd pretended not to notice and hurried on to class. I had been wondering what was going on with Justin, why he suddenly seemed interested in me, and now I knew why. I just didn't know what I thought about it yet. I had dreamed about Justin noticing me and wanting me for so long, and now it finally was happening, but I couldn't help wondering if he would have noticed if it weren't for the whole Siren thing. I mean, sure I hadn't completely transitioned yet, but my life had definitely been affected. And he hadn't said so much as a hello to me until my birthday, and since then I haven't had too much time away from him.

The idea was both depressing and exciting. Justin only wanted me because he felt uncontrollably drawn to me, but on the bright side, at least I knew for sure that I had a chance at getting him. However, as his friend, I shouldn't take advantage of the situation like that. I should try to be as fair to him as possible.

I got up and took my tray of untouched food to the trash, scanning the cafeteria for Justin.

Amanda had been talking nonstop, and was still talking to me as we walked back to our empty table, but conversations with her didn't require me to pay strict attention. The occasional nod or 'uh-huh' usually sufficed, but then she said something that caught my attention.

"Is that Justin Smith with Janie Roberts?"

"What?"

"But I thought there was something going on with you two."

I knew I was being rude, but I couldn't answer. All I could do was stare. There was Justin, my Justin, in the corner with Janie Roberts, and they were kissing.

I didn't want to watch any longer, but I found I couldn't turn away. It was like I was passing a horrific car accident, and although I didn't really want to see it, I found my eyes glued to the scene anyway.

It was an innocent kiss, as far as kisses go—Justin leaning against the wall, with Janie on the toes of her Nikes in order to reach his lips. His hands went to her hips (whether to draw her closer or push her away I couldn't be sure) and then it was over. My heart wrenched and I screamed. Well, at least I screamed in my head, but I couldn't be sure no one had heard it. My head wasn't the most private of places anymore.

Several people were watching me now, and I desperately wanted to leave before Justin found me gawking at him. With the kiss over, I found the strength to look away.

"Come on, lets get out of here," I said to Amanda before grabbing her arm and pulling her out the door with me.

☐

With two minutes left of seventh period I asked to use the bathroom. I headed straight for my car and was pulling out of the parking lot as the last bell rang. I got to Doris's before most of the other students had even reached the parking lot.

When Doris opened the door, she was wearing a bathrobe and an expectant smile.

"I want you to do it," I said.

"Come back at six tonight, and bring a bathing suit."

Chapter 11

Doris opened the door before I even had a chance to knock.

It was five minutes until six, and the sun had just dipped below the horizon, leaving the world colored in grays and blues and kind of fuzzy on the edges. There was a crispness in the air, and I was glad I'd worn my coat. It was going to be a cold night.

"Are you ready?" Doris asked, stepping out onto her porch and locking the door behind her.

"Yes, but…"

"Well, then come on. Let's get going." Doris walked to my car and turned to me impatiently.

Confused I got in and unlocked the door for her.

"Where are we going?"

"Brenda's Beauty Barn. Did you bring a bathing suit?"

I pointed mutely to a wad of spandex next to the emergency brake, and backed out onto the road.

"Good, that will make things easier," Doris continued.

A few minutes later, I parked the car in front of the closed beauty parlor.

"Will Brenda be joining us?" I asked, a little nervous, wondering what we were doing here.

Doris gave me a mischievous smile and got out of the car. I watched her for only a second before getting out myself and standing beside the car. She went over to the beauty parlor's dark window and put her face up to the glass to look in.

"I think it's closed," I said, glancing toward Highway 19 as a car drove past. Anyone driving past might think we were trying to break into the place, which made me nervous, because I wasn't sure that we weren't. I hoped we weren't. I really wasn't eager to have a criminal record.

"It was supposed to be open," Doris said, clearly frustrated.

I turned to look at Doris. How old was Doris? It was hard to say, but I'd guess she was at least in her sixties. Was that too young to be senile?

"Well, it's clearly closed. Why don't you come get into the car and we'll talk about what we're going to do."

But Doris wasn't even listening to me. She was looking under the potted plants beside the door. When she didn't find what she was looking for, she pulled up the welcome mat, then felt around the top of the doorframe.

"Are you looking for something?"

"A key," Doris said examining the doorway.

At least we weren't going to literally break in, though I didn't think the argument that we had used a key would save us in court.

"Maybe I should just…" Doris said more to herself than to me, and pulled on the door handle. The door swung open. "Ah, I should have realized."

Doris gave an embarrassed laugh and went in.

I looked around one last time to see if anyone was watching, then I followed her.

The beauty salon doubled as a gym, and the hulking free weights and exercise equipment looked ominous in the dim light. I saw movement out of the corner of my eye and gave a strangled yelp before realizing it was just my own reflection. The wall on the gym side of the building was all mirrors.

"Doris, what are we doing here?" I said in a loud whisper.

"You needn't whisper, dear, no one else is here," Doris said, her normal voice sounding loud in the big empty room.

"Doris," I pleaded.

Doris came over to me and placed her hands on my arms in a very grandmotherly way. "Oh, you're shaking. Are you alright? Sit down."

I sat down in the salon chair.

"Now, tell me what's the matter. Are you having second thoughts about the procedure?"

"The procedure? What?"

"If you want to stay *normal*, it's not my place to judge, though I wouldn't suggest it…"

"It's not that. It's this," I looked around nervously. "How can you be so calm when we could get caught any moment?"

Doris looked at me for a second then burst out laughing.

"Doris?"

Doris wiped a tear from her eye, sobering. "I'm sorry, I'm sorry. I forgot you haven't lived here very long. This used to be my place."

Seeing my less than humorous expression, Doris continued, "I mean it used to be named Doris's Place. When I retired, I let Brenda change the name, but it's still mine. I own it."

The shaking in my core calmed. "So, we're not breaking and entering?"

"For heaven's sake, no, child. No wonder you were shaking like a leaf."

"But, if this is your place, shouldn't you have a key?" I asked feeling my cheeks burning in the darkness.

"I lost it a while back, and haven't gotten around to getting a new one. I rarely come here at all."

"But, aren't you worried that Brenda will cheat you or trash the place?"

"I'm not too worried. Brenda was my business partner for many years and is like a daughter to me."

"Oh."

"So, are you okay? Are you ready to begin?" Doris asked, checking her watch.

I nodded.

"Why don't you go into one of the tanning rooms to change, while I set up? My helpers will be here shortly, and I'd like to be ready to go when they arrive."

"Okay," I mumbled, walking toward one of the three doors at the back of the room.

There was no mirror in the room, so I adjusted the swimming suit, and hoped nothing was hanging out. The little black two-piece had been bought on a whim, and now I was wishing I had bought a one piece.

A few minutes later, I shyly stepped out of the tanning room and caught my breath.

The room had been transformed. Numerous candles sitting around the room cast a soft orange glow that made the room look warm and inviting. A fountain was gurgling in the corner, and relaxing music was playing from the speakers in the ceiling. Doris had covered the window and the glass door with dark curtains, blocking out the streetlights. Now the only light came from the candles everywhere. Their warm golden light danced between the beauty parlor's mirrors and the wall of mirrors on the other side of the room, making the candles appear to go on forever in an infinite circle around the room. The room was dark enough that the candles on the tables in the center of the room seemed to be floating, little islands of light suspended in a sea of darkness. The effect was mesmerizing.

I was so focused on my surroundings that it took a few minutes to realize that Doris wasn't alone. Two other girls stood beside her, watching me, their faces in shadow.

I was suddenly very aware of how little I had on, and I tried to act casual as I approached them.

"Winter, this is Brittany Rainwater and Carrie Sullivan. Girls, this is Winter Loveless," Doris said.

Their eyes met mine and I squirmed under their gaze. This was the first time I'd seen them up close, and I took the opportunity to scrutinize them. Brittany was tall and slender, with copper skin and straight black hair that hung to her waist. Carrie was petite with a heart shaped face surrounded by a mane of soft blonde curls. They were even more beautiful then I had realized, and they were watching me curiously

"Hi," I said lamely, and gave Doris a quizzical look.

Carrie smiled revealing the most perfect teeth I'd ever seen.

She must win best smile every year, I thought.

"I thought you might want to meet a couple of the Sirens that go to school with you. They agreed to help me this week."

Other Sirens?

I know it's stupid, but the idea that there were other Sirens my age hadn't occurred to me. I looked at Brittany and Carrie with dawning wonder.

How many others were there? Am I going to look like them when Doris was done with me?

My heart quickened at the thought, whether out of fear or excitement I couldn't be sure. Then my brain finally processed what Doris had said.

"This week? How long is this process going to take?"

"Three, maybe four days. You've been blocked for a long time, and while I feel confident that I can remove the blockage completely tonight, I fear it will come back. So we'll remove it again, and again, cleansing you each time until none of the blockage remains."

"Well, let's get started."

"Don't sound so nervous, this is going to be fun," Carrie said.

Doris had me lay face up on a massage bed, and began rubbing my temples, while Brittany and Carrie arranged a collection of crystal glasses and ceramic bowls on the tables on either side of the massage bed.

"So, what do you want me to do?" I asked, feeling the need to help.

Brittany leaned close and said in a deep sultry voice, "Just lay back and enjoy. Have you ever been to a spa?"

I looked up at her towering above me. "No."

"Well, you are about to get the celebrity spa experience," Brittany said, offering a smile.

"Brittany, will you check the temperature of the stones? They should be ready by now," Doris instructed. "And, Carrie, could you mix the oil for me?"

"Sure, what oils do you want in it?" Carrie asked, going over to the table behind me. All the while, Doris continued to massage my temples and my head.

"I'm thinking grape seed, macadamia nut, and safflower oils with a few drops of lavender, rose, and sage."

I could hear the clanking of glass bottles as Carrie searched for the oils Doris wanted. Then the most amazing smells washed over me, triggering thoughts of freshly laundered sheets, warm sunny days, and newly tilled earth. I closed my eyes drinking in the fragrance.

"The stones are ready," I heard Brittany say.

I heard a few stones clank together in their water, and then felt the searing heat as the first one was placed on my chest right above my left breast, followed by one over my right breast. Then a line of stones were placed, one by one, down the middle of my abdomen, around my belly button and over each ovary. They were placed on my thighs and biceps and in each hand, before smaller stones were put on my cheeks, chin, and forehead. The heat started out nearly painful, but within seconds had become warm and comforting. Someone placed a blanket over me and my mind began to drift.

I felt the music before I heard it, a deep resonating vibration that filled my body, followed by a single piercing high note that continued uninterrupted. I opened my eyes in alarm.

"Don't be frightened," Doris's eyes seemed to say, though I couldn't actually hear what she was mouthing at me. I couldn't hear anything but that sound. The low vibrations were rolling in and out, ebbing and flowing like the sea, while the high note continued ringing in my ears, harmonizing with the low notes.

I looked over and saw Carrie running one finger around the rim of a crystal glass and Doris running some kind of stick around the inside of one of the ceramic bowls. Then Doris changed bowls and the harmony turned to dissonance, and the intensity of the sound increased.

The sound was alive inside of me, filling every inch of me, the pressure building and building. The tightness in my chest was painful. I felt like an overfilled balloon. I looked around frantically. They had to stop, it was going to kill me, but I couldn't move, couldn't breathe. My body was made of lead.

StopstopstopSTOP!

A tear ran down my cheek and into my ear, I wasn't going to last much longer.

Then I felt the pressure on my forehead give way, like the popping of a champagne cork. Brittany had removed the stone from my forehead, and released the pressure that had built up inside of me. The high ringing note ceased, though the low rumbles continued.

"Fight it. Keep playing," I heard Doris yell at Carrie, and the piercing note began again.

The sound was like a river flowing through me, like a cold drink of water on a hot summer day. It was flushing out the blockage, and leaving me feeling invigorated and clean.

Then Brittany replaced the stone on my forehead, and removed the one over my heart. When all the pressure in my chest was released and flushed out, Brittany began one by one removing the stones on my abdomen, and arms, and legs, until all my energy channels were open and clean. When my front was done, I rolled over and repeated the experience with stones that were placed down my spine and on my feet and the backs of my legs.

When the music finally stopped, I felt exhausted but happy. I could feel the change within me. I felt like an old musty attic, where someone had opened all the window and doors in order to air it out. The energy flowing through me felt cold and clean, like saline in my veins.

"Are you all right?" Doris asked. She was sweating as if she had run a race. "I know it's intense, but it will get easier."

"What was that? What did you just do?"

"It's called sound therapy. I used sound waves to break up and flush out the blockage in your Chi."

"Oh."

"I'm pooped. I think I'll go rest over on one of those mechanical massage beds for a while," Doris said wiping her brow.

"Are we done?"

"No, but Carrie and Brittany can finish up. Come and get me when you're dressed again."

"Okay."

I watched as Doris plopped down on a table a few feet from my own and slowly lay down. Then I heard a gentle hum as her table began to vibrate.

"I'll take the hair and facial, if you'll take the mani and the pedi," Carrie bartered with Brittany.

"What about the full body massage and seaweed wrap?" Brittany asked.

"We'll do those together."

"Okay by me."

I turned my attention to the two girls next to me.

"Now it's time for the fun part. So, lie back down and just relax," Brittany added in a quiet, sultry voice.

I closed my eyes and obeyed. I was tired and the sound of the fountain and the soft music were beginning to lull me to sleep. I felt Carrie and Brittany's hands on me simultaneously massaging my shoulders and my feet. Whatever tension that was left in me was soon gone.

The next two hours passed in a dreamlike haze as Carrie and Brittany pampered me head to toe. I was scrubbed, washed and beautified in every imaginable way, and in a few I'd never heard of. When they removed the warm seaweed and told me it was time to shower and get dressed again, I was surprised it was already over. It didn't feel as though enough time had passed.

Slowly, on legs that felt like jelly, I made my way to the gym's showers, where I peeled off the bikini and washed the numerous oils and creams from my body and hair. I felt lighter than I'd ever felt in my life, as if a weight had been lifted from me. I also felt…powerful. I could feel the energy

flowing through me, connecting me to…what?

I closed my eyes following the flow of energy and

found…Justin on the other end. For a second I seemed to see

him in his bedroom. He must have just gotten out of the

shower, because his hair was wet and he was wearing nothing

but a towel around his waist. I felt a shiver in the pit of my

stomach at the sight of his bare chest.

I couldn't tear my eyes away from him. His body was

hard without looking unnatural. I watched the muscles in his

back move as he walked over to his bed. He turned around to

face me, and I could see that the towel was wrapped low on

his body, exposing his hipbones and his flat stomach. But

despite how beautiful his body was, I found myself searching

his face. I admired his high cheekbones, the square of his jaw,

the way his hair was dripping into his eyes. Then he raised his head, and just as his eyes seemed to meet mine his towel dropped to the floor.

My eyes flew open. I felt like I was five years old again, walking in on him while he was on the toilet. I hadn't seen anything, but I could feel the blood rush to my cheeks.

With shaking hands, I turned off the water and stepped out of the small enclosure. By the time I had dressed and left the bathroom, I was convinced it had all been in my head.

"You look refreshed," Carrie said when I walked over to them.

"I feel amazing," I confided, smiling.

"Welcome to the family." Carrie said. Then she startled me with a big hug. "We'll see you at school tomorrow."

"Don't mind her, she's a hugger," Brittany said smiling.

Carrie stepped over to a table and began gathering her purse and coat.

"What did she mean you'll see me at school? I've never seen you guys at school," I asked Brittany.

"You're one of us now and school is going to be a lot different than it used to be. You're going to need us," Brittany said, putting on her black pea coat.

"Don't worry. Everything is going to be great, you'll see," Carrie said stifling a yawn.

"But, we need to be going. Carrie isn't much of a night person, and if we don't leave soon I'll probably have to carry her to her room, which is upstairs, and she's impossible to wake up once she completely zonks out," Brittany said.

When they had left, I walked over to where Doris lay snoring.

I hoped she would wake up easier than Carrie.

142

I nudged her. "Doris."

Doris's eyes shot open, and she looked around like a cornered rabbit, until her eyes found me. Then she sat up.

"Brittany and Carrie just left. Are you ready?"

"Yeah, just give me a minute to wake up. What time is it?"

"Nearly midnight," I said, glancing at the clock on the wall.

"Well, let's get out of here. This old lady needs to get to bed."

Chapter 12

Carrie and Brittany had warned me that school would be different, but nothing could have prepared me for just how different it was.

The next morning I got to school just before the bell rang for class, partly because I hadn't been able to tear my eyes away from my mirror. I still looked like me, only it was like the best version of me. It was what I imagined I would look like were I a supermodel in a beauty magazine—made up, airbrushed, and doctored, only I had just rolled out of bed. The other reason I was running late was nerves. It had taken me five whole minutes just to get out of my car.

What would it be like? What would people think? What would Justin think?

I walked into the senior hall with a confidence born of necessity, and it was like one of those dreams where you go to school only to realize that you forgot to put on your pants.

As I walked by, conversations stopped and people dropped what they were holding as every eye was drawn to me. I tried not to notice, while I discreetly searched the crowd for the only pair of eyes that really mattered.

When I found him, I smiled the first real smile of the morning.

He met my gaze with a warm smile of his own. I saw his eyes travel from my hair down to my feet and back to my face, but unlike the double take every other boys had made as I passed he simply watched me approach, looking at me no differently than he had every day in the past week. There was no jaw dropping, no drooling, no need to straighten his own clothes or adjust his hair. And I wasn't sure if I was pleased or disappointed by that.

Then I was standing right in front of him, and I realized that I didn't know what to say. He wasn't proclaiming his undying love for me as he had in several scenarios I'd imagined. He was just acting like Justin, which was both comforting and disconcerting.

"Hi," I said lamely.

"Hey," Justin said, his fingers brushing against my own sending a jolt right through me. I felt like I hadn't talked to Justin in years, though it had only been a day.

"Hi, Winter."

I turned and saw, for the first time, Janie Roberts standing next to Justin. Though her smile was inviting, her eyes were anything but, and after sizing me up, she stepped closer to Justin and laid her hand on his arm possessively.

146

"Hi, Janie, I didn't see you there," I said as pleasantly as possible, suddenly remembering why I hadn't talked to Justin yesterday.

"Justin and I are going to the Harvest Ball this weekend," Janie confided as if we were best friends, though I knew she was just gloating.

"So, I've heard," I said, matching her tone, though I couldn't help glancing up at Justin when I said it.

"Have you asked anyone yet?" Janie asked, her voice syrupy sweet.

"No, I'm more of an old-fashioned girl. I prefer for the guy to ask me," I said with mock friendliness.

"Well, you better not wait too long, or all the good ones will be taken. FYI I heard that Billy Thompson still hasn't ask anyone yet."

"Thanks for the tip, but I think I'd rather just *be alone*." As I repeated Justin's words, I dropped all friendly pretenses.

Then the bell rang, rescuing me from the uncomfortable silence, and I rushed off to my first class. I didn't look back, but I swear I could feel Justin's eyes following me until I disappeared into Mr. Pruitt's room.

Word that I was waiting to be asked out traveled fast, and by lunchtime eight different boys had asked me to the Harvest Ball. I'd also had two invitations to go cruising, whatever that meant, though I had a feeling it entailed more parking than driving.

I had been brought up to have manners, and probably would have said yes to the first boy who asked me to the dance out of sheer politeness, had our conversation not been interrupted by the second boy, at which point I had simply walked away.

I walked to lunch, avoiding eye contact with those around me, fearing that that alone would give others the confidence they needed to approach me. After I paid for my food I was heading for my seat across from Amanda when I realized that Justin, and much to my surprise Janie, were sitting with her.

That seat was out. There was no way I was going to sit next to *them* for all of lunch. Then, as I was searching the cafeteria for another seat, ignoring the numerous boys trying to get my attention, I saw them.

Carrie and Brittany had a table to themselves outside in the courtyard. Despite the frigid temperatures, the tables around them were filled with girls and boys, who looked as though they wished they could join them.

Nervously, I approached.

"This seat taken?"

"Winter! Sit down," Carrie said welcomingly.

"So, how's your day going so far?" Brittany asked knowingly.

As irritating as the constant male attention had felt at the time, I couldn't help smiling.

"That good, eh?"

"Well, yesterday I was invisible, and today I've had ten different boys ask me out."

"Have you said yes to any of them? All of them?" Brittany asked.

I blushed. "No."

"You'll have to excuse Brittany. She's a chain dater," Carrie said.

"A what?"

"She says yes to everybody," Carrie explained.

Wide eyed I looked at Brittany.

"What? It's one of the perks of our…condition. Besides, I don't say yes to just everybody. I'm just not as picky as Carrie. She believes in true love, and soul mates, and all that crap."

"I just haven't found that someone special yet, and if I want to wait till I do, that's my choice," Carrie said, blushing.

"Is it getting warmer out here or is it just me?" I ask fanning myself, and taking off my jacket.

"That would be Brittany," Carrie said quieter, so none of the other tables could hear. "You can always tell when she gets worked up. Watch out if she gets mad at you, you're likely to get struck by lightning."

"I've never hit anyone with lightning, I do have *some* control. Maybe a little hail every now and then, but never lightning."

"You can control the weather?" I supposed it wasn't any weirder than my ability to send psychic subliminal messages. "Really?"

"Yeah. I was kidding about the hail, though. Mostly all I can do is mess with the temperature."

"That's cool. What about you, Carrie? Are you gifted?"

"I can talk to animals."

"Like in that movie?" I blurted out, and instantly regretted it. I may as well have just said, "Hi, I'm a dork".

Carrie smiled, unoffended. "Kind of."

"So, both of you are gifted," I paused, trying to remember the term Doris had used, "But I thought that wasn't very common."

"It's not, but several of us in this area are. It has to do with the location. The only thing that can contain our voices is earth. So, the stronger Sirens tend to live in the interior of the country near entrances to deep caverns, while the weaker Sirens and the Graces have mostly migrated to the places like L. A., New York, and Beverly Hills."

"Most of the strongest Sirens live in Missouri, actually. Though there is a group that lives in New Mexico," Brittany chimed in.

"Wait, what's a Grace?"

"Graces are Sirens that aren't Gifted and don't have the voice," Carrie said.

"Kind of like second class Sirens," Brittany added.

"Isn't that kind of harsh?" I asked.

"Once you've lived in our world longer you'll understand. It seems harsh, but Graces and Sirens don't really associate with each other, even though technically we are sisters. They think we are freaks because of the things we can do, and we know they're just weaker," Carrie said.

"Hey, don't be bashing my kind to the new girl," said a voice behind me.

I turned and saw a miniature version of Brittany behind me.

"Hi, I'm Cami, Brittany's little sister," the girl said, extending her hand.

I shook it. "I'm Winter."

"Don't you have a class to get to or something? Freshmen aren't allowed to eat yet," Brittany said, glaring at her sister.

"Most Freshmen can't, but when you look like this you get all kinds of special treatment," Cami said.

"So, your sister is a Grace? How's that?" I asked.

"It's so weird how new you are to this," Cami exclaimed, staring at me like I was a rare specimen.

"Shut up," Brittany said.

"A Siren's first child is always a Siren, or at least carries the Siren power to be passed down to posterity (if it's a boy, which is very rare). Any children she has beyond that are Graces, blessed with her beauty but none of her powers. And their children in turn are Graces and so on. But Sirens don't often have more than one child. When her powers are transferred to her daughter, the spell the father was in breaks, and if it wasn't true love he usually leaves. I don't know why, but crones, or Sirens who have passed on their powers, usually don't ever remarry.

155

"Oh," I said, feeling dumb.

"So, there you have it," Carrie said, then turning to Brittany added, "and you wonder why I want to find the real thing. Aren't you worried about that at all?"

"No, not really," Brittany said casually.

"So, do you have any cool abilities?" Cami asked, between slurps on the blow pop she had brought with her.

Carrie and Brittany hadn't asked, but they were clearly interested in what I could do.

"I can telepathically influence people," I said. I had spent hours trying to find a way to describe what I could do in a way that didn't sound horrible.

"Like mind control?" Brittany said.

I don't know why I even tried. "Yeah."

"That explains something I'd been wondering about last night," Carrie said.

156

"I'm sorry about that. I wasn't sure if I'd done anything or not, but I guess now I know. Do you mind if I ask you something?" When they both nodded, I continued. "What did it feel like? It didn't hurt, did it?"

"No, it didn't hurt," Carrie reassured me.

"I didn't even realize you had done anything," Brittany said.

"If it hadn't been for what Doris said, I wouldn't have known that you had done anything either. It had felt like my own thoughts or really strong intuition. I was playing the crystal, and I suddenly felt this pressing urge to stop, so I did. Usually I can trust my intuition." Carrie sounded a little uncomfortable.

"Have you tried using it on anyone today?" Brittany asked.

"Not on purpose, though I think it's my fault Mr. Cox didn't give my class a quiz. I've heard that he gave every other class a quiz. Actually, ever since I discovered my...talent, I've been trying to *not* use it. I just don't feel right about it. I guess that's going to be harder to do now."

Carrie nodded.

Brittany rolled her eyes. "Whatever. I think it's cool."

I wasn't sure I agreed, but I still appreciated Brittany saying it, and I gave her a grateful smile.

"So, you have to come with us to the Harvest Ball," Carrie said, changing the subject.

"Not you too! Everyone is obsessed with this dance," I said exasperated.

"I just like any opportunity to dress up, but a lot of people are just worried about the local superstition."

"What's that? I haven't heard anything."

"There are only two formal dances: the Harvest Ball and Prom. Prom of course is the most important, but there is this local superstition that whatever happens at the Harvest Ball determines how your Prom will go."

"Meaning?"

"Whomever you take to the Harvest Ball will be your date for the Prom in the spring, and if you go stag, you won't be able to get a date for the Prom."

"What if you just skip the dance all together?" I asked.

"If you don't attend, something terrible will happen that will keep you from going to Prom."

I looked at Carrie and Brittany skeptically. "Do you really believe any of that?"

"I don't know. But I'd rather go just to be safe," Carrie said.

"What do you mean by that?"

"Angie Somerset, Jaclyn Bird, and Sarah Jones were best friends. They were seniors last year. They were all artsy types, liked to dress weird and generally go against the crowd. Well since it was their last year, they decided to take a stand and not go to the dance. They held this party on the same night as the Harvest Ball and invited all of their friends, so they all skipped the Harvest Ball. Then, a couple days before the Prom, the Art Club took a trip to St. Louis and the bus got into an accident. Nobody was killed, but everyone who went to that party was injured and missed the Prom," Brittany ended matter-of-factly.

I looked at her incredulously and rolled my eyes. "Coincidence."

"Then two years ago, there was this boy named Jack. He was really uncool and instead of going alone, decided to not go at all. Then, later in the year, he started dating this girl and they were going to go to Prom together, only he got killed in a car accident on the way to pick her up for Prom," Brittany said.

They were both just looking at me, but I didn't know what to say. It didn't feel right to make light of someone dying. "I don't have a dress."

"What are you, a size four? I'm sure I could find something suitable for you to wear," Carrie said.

"Fine, I'll go, but I still don't believe any of it," I said.

"Yea! We can meet at my house at ten to get ready," Carrie.

"In the morning? The dance isn't until seven."

Carrie smiled and nodded.

"P.M.," I added in case she hadn't understood me.

"You want to look your best, don't you?" Carrie asked.

"I guess," I said.

161

"Don't worry, it'll be fun," Carrie said smiling.

I said okay, but I was still wary. Nine hours was a long time to get ready.

"Now we have to find you a date," Brittany said.

"I'd really rather go alone."

"Now what is so wrong with these boys, that you can't enjoy a night of dancing with them?" Brittany asked.

"Nothing, it's just…"

"There's someone else," Carrie said. It wasn't a question.

"Yeah, but he's going with someone else," I said, not meeting their eyes. I felt pathetic admitting it.

"Well, nothing gets a man's attention like jealousy," Brittany said.

Jealousy. Would Justin get jealous if I went with someone else?

"Brittany, not everyone is like you," Carrie was saying.

"You're right," I said, interrupting her, looking at Brittany.

"Winter, you don't have to. I don't have a date yet. I'd be glad to go stag with you," Carrie said.

"No, I'll get a date. Are we going to have them pick us up at your house, Carrie?"

Carrie looked at me for a second, shrugged, and said, "Okay. Tell your dates to meet us at my house and we'll all share a limo over to the dance."

The bell for fifth hour rang, and I got up and threw away my trash.

"So, I'll see you guys tonight?" I asked them.

"Yeah, see you."

Chapter 13

Getting a date wasn't hard. But finding someone I wanted or was willing to spend that much time with was. And as the day worn on, I seemed to have fewer and fewer prospects. My chi was blocked again, just like Doris said.

After school, on the way to my car, Justin stopped me. I hadn't seen him since lunch, and it figured that he would show up now, when I was back to normal again.

"Winter, wait up."

I stopped in the middle of the sidewalk and waited for Justin to catch up. When he did, he took my very heavy backpack and put it on his shoulder.

"What do you have in here, rocks?"

"I have a lot of homework."

"Do you need any help with it? I could come over tonight."

I knew it was more an offer to spend time with me than to help me with my Algebra II assignment, and I smiled.

"I'd love it if you could help, but I'm not going to be able to get to my homework till pretty late tonight. I've got plans this evening."

Justin held my arm, turning me to look up at him.

"Who's the lucky guy?"

The question sounded casual, even friendly, but there was something in his eyes that said otherwise. And as much as I wanted to make him jealous, make him know how it felt every time I saw him and Janie together, I couldn't lie.

"Actually, I have plans with Brittany Rainwater and Carrie Sullivan." *Besides, what would* Janie *think about you coming over?*

165

"Oh, I didn't realize you were friends."

"It's kind of new," I conceded. *Kind of like you and Janie.*

Justin smiled as though he thought that was funny. "Well, as long as you don't forget your old friends."

I grabbed his hand and squeezed it, igniting a fire in my fingers. I wondered if he noticed how warm my hand suddenly was or if it just felt that way to me. "I'll never forget you." *I love you.*

Justin looked as though he wanted to say something, but stopped himself.

"So, it looks as though I'll be seeing you and Janie at the dance after all," I said, breaking the silence and taking my hand out of his.

"Decided to grace us commoners with your presence?" he said, mocking me, the tension between us gone for the moment.

I nudged him playfully. "Yeah, I don't really want to break my arm or anything this spring."

"What?"

"Are you saying you've never heard of the Harvest Ball Curse?"

"Sure, I have. I just never though of you as the superstitious type."

"If you think I'll be okay, I guess I could miss it…"

"I didn't say that," Justin said.

"So, you do believe in the curse."

"You got me. Totally superstitious." Justin smiled. "I'll save you a dance."

Butterflies took flight in my stomach. "Is Janie going to allow that?"

"It's not her decision. I'm sorry about the way she was talking to you this morning."

"Oh, you picked up on that, did you?"

"She's just jealous," Justin said, his voice sounding like it had outside my apartment on my birthday.

Shocked, I searched his face. "Of what, my GPA?"

"You're right, maybe she's the one I should be tutoring?" Justin said, playful again, all huskiness gone from his voice.

We were at my car. And I found myself wishing the conversation didn't have to end.

"Have fun tonight."

"You too," I said sadly, imagining who he might spend it with.

I got into my car, throwing the backpack Justin had handed back to me into the passenger seat, and cranked up the heat. It was really cold for October. I watched Justin jog across the parking lot to his car, admiring his butt and the curve of his back. Then I pulled out of the parking lot and headed home.

That night was much the same as the night before. I took Doris over to Brenda's Beauty Barn, where Carrie and Brittany met us. They unblocked my chi with sound therapy, and Carrie and Brittany pampered me afterward, though much to my disappointment not as much as the night before.

When Brittany told me to go take a shower after my massage and full body mud mask were finished, my disappointment must have been obvious.

"Sweetie, most spa treatments aren't meant to be used daily. It wouldn't be good for your skin," Carrie said, her dimples showing.

I knew she was probably right, so I reluctantly headed for the bathroom. When I got into the shower, I forgot my desire to be anywhere but there. The hot water felt wonderful as it melted away the remains of my mud mask. Once I was clean, I took a moment to just enjoy the silky caress of the water as it soothed my muscles and cleared my mind.

I could feel the energy flowing unhindered inside of me, through me. Once again, I felt that invisible string tethering me to Justin. When I focused on it I realized I could feel a tugging in the connection that told me where he was, and I was even vaguely aware of what he was doing—as if I'd telepathically low-jacked him. It was unbelievably cool and disconcerting at the same time.

Justin's connection to me felt like his caress, electric and magical. I closed my eyes reveling in the feeling and there he was, sitting in his kitchen. Startled I opened my eyes again and the vision was gone; all I saw was the shower in front of me. Curious I closed my eyes again, and I was back in Justin's kitchen with him. It was as if in my mind, behind my eyelids was a window that let me see him. Part of me wondered if I could see other people as well, but not enough to try.

He was sitting at the table leaning over a textbook. His hair was slightly mussed as if he'd been running his fingers through it. He was doing his homework and I swear it was just about the sexiest thing I'd ever seen. (Just about—because the night before I'd seen him in just a towel.)

You know you have it bad when homework is sexy, but it was. I moved in a little closer until I was sitting (hovering? watching?) right next to him. I wanted so badly to reach out and touch him, but I held back. I wasn't sure how this worked or what would happen if I did.

Then I saw him turn, hearing some noise I could not. He got up and I followed him to the front door. He opened it to reveal Janie standing demurely on his porch. I gasped and Justin looked in my direction, but my attention was focused on Janie. She was talking and gesturing into the house, but I couldn't hear any of it. It was only then that I realized how silent this entire vision had been, and the one before it.

So, I could see but not hear?

I opened my eyes, feeling as though I were being dragged backward through a tunnel, and then I was just in the shower. I wondered if I were to close my eyes, if I'd see Justin again, but I'd seen enough. Though I tried to avoid it, I was able to see that little budding romance every day in the halls, in the cafeteria, at school in general, why would I torture myself and watch it in my head as well.

I turned off the water, eager to escape.

I found Brittany and Carrie waiting for me on the couch in the salon's waiting area. Doris had fallen asleep again. I sat down.

"Are you ever overwhelmed by it all?" I asked nobody in particular.

"It gets better," Carrie said sympathetically. There was silence as we were all lost in our own thoughts for a few minutes. As I tried to calm the shaking in my stomach and embrace what was happening to me, I wondered absentmindedly what Carrie and Brittany were thinking about.

They both answered simultaneously.

"Will I ever find true love? I mean the feelings we invoke in men, are just an illusion, a spell. How will I ever know if it is real? I don't want to end up like my mother, raising a daughter alone because the man I thought loved me leaves me when the spell is broken," Carrie said.

"I wonder who Winter will take to the dance. I hope she picks someone soon," Brittany said.

Carrie seemed surprised she had spoken her thought aloud, but it wasn't until her shocked eyes found my own that I realized what had happened. I felt like I was going to vomit.

"I'm sorry. I was just wondering…I'm so sorry. I didn't mean…" I spluttered, on the verge of tears.

"Did you do that? That was awesome. But next time give a girl a heads-up before I blab my brains out to whoever is within hearing range. There are some things a girl wants to keep to hersef," Brittany said, smiling with wonder at me.

"It's okay," Carrie's eyes were now forgiving. "I know. It takes time to learn how to deal with it. I remember a time shortly after I started being able to talk to animals. I had gone to the zoo on a class trip, and while I was sitting on a bench, a woman behind me asked me where we were from and I told her. It wasn't until I saw the confused expressions of my friends that I realized that the only thing behind me was the Giraffe cage, and that I'd just spoken Giraffe in front of everyone. Now I'm more cautious."

"I'm still sorry." Then I turned to Brittany. "Brittany, why on earth do you want me to get a date so badly?"

"It thought it would be obvious. So, I can have the rest of the guys to myself. I don't want to take someone you're after. I'm more about quantity than quality. So, do you have a date yet?"

"No, I'm working on it," I said, blushing.

"Who is he?" Carrie asked.

"Who's who?"

"The one who's got you blushing like that?"

"Justin Smith," I admitted.

"He's yummy, so what are you waiting for? Go tell him to take you or whatever it is you do," Brittany said, glancing at Carrie then back at me.

"I want him to be with me because he wants to, not because I made him."

"Believe me, Winter, he *wants* you," Brittany said, giving me a meaningful look. "And so does every able bodied male in the area. I know this is new to you, but you are a Siren. They all want you."

"You don't understand. I've been in love with him since I was nine years old. I've been dreaming of him, of *us*, my whole life. I don't want him to want me because of this stupid Siren thing; I want him to want *me*."

176

"No, Winter, you want him to *love* you, and that isn't something we can make anyone do. Sure, we can make them *want* us, but *love*…we have to find that just like anyone else," Carrie said, her voice sad.

I wondered if Carrie had a somebody she wasn't talking about, but I kept that thought to myself, or at least I think I did; I can never really be sure. But there was something I wanted to know.

"But what happens if a Siren has a boy? Are there boy Sirens walking around?"

Carrie still seemed far away, lost in thought, so Brittany answered my question.

"Sirens can have boys, in fact Doris has a son, though we've never met him. But it is very rare to have a boy. Something about our genetic make up makes us have girls somehow. I don't know, maybe our uteruses are boy sperm haters, and they only let the girls through," Brittany said smiling.

"Feminist uteruses," I said, envisioning it in my head.

Brittany chuckled. "Whatever the reason, it's very rare to have a boy. And when we do, he doesn't get any of the Siren abilities, except maybe the looks. Other than that he's just a carrier and passes it on to his daughter. At least that's what's I've heard. I've never met one myself."

There was a pause in the conversation, and I saw Carrie stifle a yawn.

"It's getting late, we should probably get going," Brittany said.

"Remember that it's just a dance. Go get a date and have fun. It doesn't have to be love," Carrie said.

"If you don't get a date soon, I'll get one for you," Brittany threatened.

"That won't be necessary. I'll get one," I said.

"You better," Brittany said, giving me a mischievous smile. "Because I guarantee you won't like anyone I pick for you."

"We'll see you tomorrow," Carrie said, yawning again.

After they left I looked at the clock, and was surprised it was only nine o'clock. Wow, Carrie really isn't a night person.

Doris's quiet snoring drifted to me from the massage table she was sleeping on, and suddenly I just really wanted to go home and do my homework.

Chapter 14

"Did you hear about that girl from Rolla?"

I was in Biology the next morning, and had just sat down. Realizing he was talking to me, I turned around to look at the boy who sat behind me. Collin Greene was the smartest kid in my Bio class, and possibly in my graduating class. He and I had been on friendly terms since the beginning of school, though I wouldn't exactly call us friends. Most of our conversations had revolved around biology and homework assignments. He was just the type of person who was friendly with everyone.

I studied his blue eyes through the dark frames of his glasses, then let my gaze take in his blonde hair and relatively clear skin.

I could take him to the dance.

He was no Justin, but he was one of the few boys at school with whom I could imagine spending a couple of hours without wanting to kill either him or myself.

"Did you hear about the girl from Rolla?" He asked again.

"Yeah, it's terrible."

Yeah, I knew. It had been all over the news last night, and not just the local ones. It had been on every channel last night when I hadn't been able to sleep.

A college student attending UMR had been murdered, and while murder wasn't unheard of in Rolla, it was usually caused by domestic disputes, or drugs, or both. This one was different. Her body had been found by the banks of the Little Piney River, and though they weren't releasing details about how she was killed, they had said that it was similar to eight other bodies that had been found along the Mississippi and Missouri Rivers in the past twelve months.

"They're saying it looks like a serial killer," Collin said.

"It's scary," I said.

I regretted the thought I'd had earlier about killing boys. Now it just didn't seem appropriate. Here I was, nine people had been murdered, and all I could think about was how do I shift this conversation so I could ask him to the dance on Saturday. I supposed I could just make him ask me, but that didn't seem appropriate either.

"So, Collin, this is kind of off the subject," I said, trying to not sound as nervous as I felt. "but, are you going to the dance this Saturday?"

Collin smiled. "Maybe. It depends on who's asking?"

"I'm asking, and you aren't making it any easier," I said, encouraged by his smile, and the fact that if this didn't turn out the way I planned, I could just make him take me to the dance.

"Are you asking if I'm going, or if I'd like to go with *you*?"

I couldn't believe it. He was trying to make me squirm on purpose, but it was actually having the opposite effect. If anything, the way he was teasing me, was just making me feel more comfortable with him. Though he was clearly interested, he was keeping control of himself, playing with me, making me work for it. Any other boy would have been drooling by now. It was only the second day of full Siren status, and it was kind of scary how quickly I'd gotten used to boys doing whatever I wanted them to. Except for Justin, but I didn't want to think about that.

I rolled my eyes. "Collin, would you please go to the dance with me?"

"Well, if you're going to beg," Collin said.

"Come to Carrie Sullivan's house around six-thirty. We're all going to share a limo." I might have said more, but the tardy bell rang and Mr. Pruitt, who liked to use up every second of his class time, had already begun his lecture on Mendel and his bean plants.

Of course, because I was trying to not think about Justin, he was the only thing on my mind, and I thought I could almost feel him sitting in his Spanish class down the hall.

□

"I got a date for Saturday," I said, putting down my lunch tray next to Carrie's.

"So, who's the lucky guy?" Brittany asked.

"Collin Greene."

"Who's that?" Brittany asked.

"A boy in my bio class. He's smart and nice," I said, feeling defensive.

"So, are you giving up on Justin?" Carrie asked.

"Not exactly, but like you said, it's just a dance. It's not like I'm marrying the guy."

"Good, because we both got dates too," Carrie said, "and I was going to feel bad if you still didn't have one, since I said I'd go by myself with you."

"You did say you'll have a dress for me, didn't you?"

"Yes, I've got several you can choose from," Carrie said.

"What about hair and makeup?"

"Don't worry, you're going to look great," Brittany said, and Carrie beamed at me.

"Good."

"I thought you said it was just a dance. Why the sudden interest to look your best for this boy?" Brittany asked.

"Because, Justin will be at the dance and said he'd save me a dance. And I intend on holding him to that promise."

"Winter's going to steal her a man," Brittany said, as if she were a proud parent.

☐

There was one good thing about being able to sense Justin's presence—it was easy to avoid him. Well, easy to know where he was, but it was decidedly harder not to use that knowledge to go toward him. Even across the school campus,

I could feel the magnetic pull of his body on mine. The invisible connection between us felt vaguely like his touch, but just enough to tease and tempt me to want more. The truth was, it was torture to avoid him, but I needed to get through it for one more day. That night I would have my third and, hopefully, final sound therapy cleansing, after which I would be a fully operational Siren. My hope was that once my energy was unblocked, that magnetic pull would work both ways, drawing Justin to me as much I was drawn to him.

Chapter 15

That night Doris opened the door before I had a chance to knock, and I was surprised to see her dressed in a gray sweater and long black skirt. Gone were her dangling earrings and bangle bracelets. In fact, everything about her looked darker, muted.

"Doris?"

"Are you ready to go?"

"Yes."

"Then let's go."

Doris brushed by me and got into the car without another word. I wanted to ask what was wrong, but knew that Doris would tell me when she was ready, if it was something she wanted me to know.

We drove down through town in silence until we got to Highway 19, and Doris told me to take a left.

"But the salon is that way," I said.

"We're not going to the salon tonight."

"But I thought you were going to do another sound therapy session with me."

"Just turn left."

I turned left. We followed the highway until we'd left the lights of town far behind us. The highway seemed to stretch out forever before us, and just when I was beginning to wonder if Doris had fallen asleep, she had me turn right onto a little dirt road. As we wound our way through the trees, I hoped she knew where we were going, because I sure as heck didn't. The road eventually ended in a dead end, either that or the trees pressing close to the road had overtaken it. To my surprise, there were several other cars parked randomly at the end of the road and along the tree line. I found a space that I hoped I could get out of later and shut off the engine.

"Doris, what are we doing?"

"We're having a Sing for the family of Shyla Belter," Doris said.

"Who's Shyla...you mean the girl who was killed?" I felt a chill run down my spine.

"Yes, she was a Siren."

"Oh," I said, getting out of the car after Doris.

I followed Doris down a small dirt path that led into the woods from the makeshift parking lot. The canopy of leaves above us blocked out the bright moonlight, and I had to grab a tree trunk every few minutes to keep from tripping over unseen limbs and potholes in the path. I was happy when we finally broke through the tree line, and a riverbank opened up in front of us.

190

The ground in front of us was dark, and sloped steeply down to the river where mist hung like a ghost above the water. A sandy beach shown like silver in the moonlight on the far bank, which sloped steadily upward, and I thought I could just make out an outcropping of rocks half way up the hill.

Without hesitation, Doris made her way down the riverbank to the remains of a low water bridge to our right. The mass of broken concrete still connected the two banks, though its pieces lay haphazardly in the water. Cautiously, I followed Doris across to the opposite bank, hoping that there were no snakes living in the dark crevices.

The climb up to the outcropping of rock was steep, and by the time we reached it our breath was coming out in little clouds around us in the cold damp air. I was surprised to see that between the rocks was the opening to a cave. When we had caught our breath, I followed Doris into the cave, feeling along the wall in the darkness.

The floor of the cave sloped steadily down into the hill in a straight path for about twenty yards, before it turned sharply to the left. We walked about five more feet and turned sharply to the right and into a cavern about the size of my apartment if there were no interior walls. The room was lit by a combination of candles and twinkle lights, which looked bright in comparison to the blackness of the tunnel behind me.

Along the far wall a large rock structure created a natural stage, and in front of the stage, sitting in pews made of rocks and plywood, were about fifteen women, all of which turned to stare at us when we entered.

The first thing I noticed was that sitting toward the back of the room, just a few feet from where I stood, were Brittany and Carrie, next to two women who could only be their mothers. They waved me over to them and I willingly obliged, while Doris went to sit next to a woman dressed all in black at the front of the room.

The room filled with quiet chatter as Doris and I found our seats.

"Carrie, what's going on?" I asked Carrie, who was sitting next to me.

"Didn't Doris explain on the way over?"

"Doris didn't say much of anything on the way over."

"We're having a Sing," Carrie said, as though I should know what she was talking about.

"Yeah, Doris said that too, but I don't have a clue what either of you is talking about."

"I forgot that your momma didn't teach you any of this. We have Sings for lots of different reasons. It's our way of expressing ourselves to one another in the way that only Sirens can. Tonight, we sing for a fallen Siren."

"So, we're having a funeral?"

"Kind of, you'll see."

I looked around at the benches and lighting. "This cave looks like a bizarre underground church. I mean it doesn't look as though this was an impromptu meeting."

"You remember what I told you about earth being the only thing that can contain our power? Well, Doris's son wired this place for her back in the sixties, and we have been using it ever since. Underground is the one place we don't have to hold back. We're lucky, not every group's cave is as nice as this one," Carrie whispered.

"So how does this work?"

"Shh, they're starting," Carrie said, her attention on the stage.

Doris had taken the stage and was waiting for everyone to quiet down.

"It is always a tragedy when a young person dies, but we feel it even harder when it's one of our own. Shyla wasn't from around here. She had come here from out east to go to college. She had dreams of becoming a veterinarian, but now those dreams will never be realized."

The woman on the front row, Shyla's mother, dissolved into sobs, and another woman moved over to comfort her.

"Now," Doris continued, "we will say goodbye in true Siren fashion—with song." Doris looked at Shyla's mother, gave a short nod and left the stage.

A few moments later Mrs. Belter climbed the stairs leading to the stage, blotting her swollen eyes. I looked on curiously.

"Shyla was the best person I know, and I know most of you never got to meet her. But I would appreciate it if you would sing with me tonight," the woman said, her voice quavering. Then she began to sing.

Goose bumps broke out on my arms, at the sound of her voice. She sang about her daughter, about loss, and finally about new beginnings. As the power of her voice washed over me, I could feel how she felt. I was in a sea of grief and sorrow for the loss of a person I'd never met. When her song came to an end, and the emotions receded, I was surprised to find my face wet with my own tears.

When Shyla's mother left the stage, she was a completely different woman than when she had gone up there. It was as if a burden had been lifted from her. We had shared in her grief, and she was lighter because of it.

Then Doris returned to the stage. "Tina, I'm truly sorry for your loss," she said to Mrs. Belter, and then her eyes found me. "Winter Loveless, would you please join me on stage?"

Startled, I looked to Brittany and Carrie for approval before, shyly standing up and making my way up to the front of the room, and onto the stage.

"Winter is new to our group. This is her first Sing, and as is our custom she will now sing for us, her first Siren song."

My heart jumped into my throat.

I'm going to do what?

"Doris," I whispered, as if everyone else might not notice me, "what are you doing? I don't know what I'm supposed to do."

"Just sing from your heart," Doris whispered back, and everyone else laughed.

I pulled her aside, standing close so no one would hear. "What about my blocked energy? Won't that make a difference?" I sincerely hoped it would.

"I was going to take care of that before your first Sing, but I think singing will do the job." Doris looked at me appraisingly. "There doesn't seem to be much left blocking your chakras anyway."

"But…"

"Sing, Winter. Cleanse yourself from the inside out," Doris said.

"But I didn't even know Shyla," I protested.

"You don't have to sing about her. Sing from your heart about you and whatever you are going through, and we will all share in it and bear it with you. Don't worry, we will each take our turn up here tonight. You are not alone." Then Doris left the stage.

Rather than look at all of the faces staring expectantly up at me, I closed my eyes and thought about what Doris had said. What was in my heart? What burden did I need lifted?

I opened my mouth, and a song began flowing, as if by magic, from my lips. With my eyes closed I let every thought and emotion I'd kept locked away wash over me. As I sang, the air filled with all the melancholy, loneliness, and bittersweet hope I'd been feeling since my mother's accident. The feelings were so strong they seemed tangible, and I opened my eyes half-expecting to see my mother lying, broken in her hospital bed. To my surprise, it looked as though every one present felt the same way. It was then that I realized that I wasn't singing about how I felt, but that my song was the feelings themselves, brought to life by the power of my voice. Then my thoughts turned to Justin and the haunting melody of the lament I'd been singing shifted seamlessly into a ballad filled with all the excitement and angst of first love. When the last intoxicating notes of my melody had faded, there wasn't a dry eye in the cave.

When I finally sat down, Doris came over and sat beside me.

"How do you feel?" Doris asked.

Wiping the tears from my eyes, I took a moment to really think about it. I felt, light and free and invigorated and clean and I told her so.

"Winter, you are whole again. The canker inside of you has been removed." Then Doris patted my knee, the way I always imagined a grandmother would, and I couldn't contain my smile.

She was right. I had been so caught up in the experience of singing and really being heard, that I hadn't noticed what was happening to me. But I could feel it now.

The power within me felt like a raging river, bursting at the seams, held back by will power alone. All my energy channels where open now and nothing else was blocking the way.

Chapter 16

After everyone had sang, Doris took me around to introduce me to the other Sirens. I was extremely nervous, and managed to only accidentally influence two people. But they didn't seem to notice, and I wasn't about to tell them.

Of course, I already knew Carrie and Brittany, and I had become acquainted with their mothers Nancy Sullivan and Hazel Rainwater between songs. I didn't get the opportunity to meet Tina Belter, because as soon as the Sing was done she had slipped out unannounced, but we all understood. We had all felt her pain, and I'd probably have done the same thing if I were in her shoes.

First, Doris introduced me to her daughter Brenda, who seemed to have heard a lot about me. There were three other girls close to my age. Sarah, who was from Eminence, was a junior like me and had come with her mother, Gretchen, and her grandmother, Rose. Austin and Caitlyn were both seniors from Viburnnum, and were there with their mothers as well.

In fact, there were only two other women who were alone like me—Prudence and Beth. Prudence was an elderly lady, with a hunched back and a walker. Her daughter had moved to Texas, and she hadn't seen her or her granddaughter in years. Beth was about my mother's age. She was dressed as if she had just gotten off work before coming, and she told me her mother had died several years previous and that she had never had a daughter.

I instantly felt a kinship with both of them, especially Beth. I knew what it was like to be alone. I was curious what Beth did and what her life was like, but Carrie and Brittany stole me away before I could find out.

"Your song was beautiful," Carrie said.

"Yours too, both of you," I said, looking between Carrie and Brittany.

"So, what did you think?" Brittany asked.

"It was the most amazing thing I've ever experienced," I answered honestly.

Brittany smiled suggestively. "I wouldn't say it's the most amazing thing *I've* experienced, but it was pretty cool."

Carrie rolled her eyes at Brittany. "You are such a whore," she said, but she was smiling.

Brittany just smiled, and examined her manicure.

"So, did you ask Doris whether we're going to meet at her house tomorrow for another sound therapy?" Carrie asked.

"Actually, I'm not going to need one," I said beaming. "Tonight's music seems to have done the trick."

"Really? Yea! Although, it was nice getting together so often," Carrie said.

I couldn't believe it. She, one of the most sweet, gorgeous, country girls I'd ever met was worried I wouldn't have time for her. "Don't worry, we'll still hang out."

"Promise?" Carrie said.

"Yeah, besides I'll be at your house Saturday," I reminded her.

"I hate to cut our little after school special short, but Carrie and I need to get going," Brittany said.

"I should be leaving too. Let me find Doris and we could all walk out together. Neither of us brought a flashlight. Did either of you?"

"I have one." Brittany held up a pink maglight.

"You are a lifesaver."

I found Doris still talking to Brenda, and soon we were heading back out into the cold night, guided by the light of Brittany's flashlight.

I shivered, wrapping my jacket tighter. "Brittany, can't you do something about the cold."

"You know, it's not as simple as that to manipulate the weather," Brittany said, but it seemed to get a bit warmer after that.

Chapter 17

On Thursday morning, I stood examining myself in the mirror. It was early, the sun wasn't quite up, but I was too excited to sleep any longer. I couldn't believe how good I looked. My hair had bounce and shine. My teeth looked whiter and straighter, and my skin seemed to glow from within. I was beautiful.

There was no way Justin wouldn't want me. Today was the day I would finally have him.

I took a long time debating what I should wear. I wanted something that would say, 'Hey, look at me', but none of my clothes were made to stand out. I decided on my favorite jeans (they were comfortable and made my butt look good), and a plain black t-shirt. (I'd been too scared to wear it before, for fear it would make me look like the living dead.

But the way I looked now, I was pretty sure I could wear a paper bag and make it look good.)

I was on my way out when my phone rang. I thought about letting the machine get it, but gave in and ran to get it.

"Hello?"

"Hey, I got you before you left."

My heart gave a little flutter at the sound of Justin's voice.

"Hey."

"Winter, could you do me a favor?"

"What's that?" I asked

"I'm going to be gone for the next two days, and I was hoping you would get my homework for me, so I can do it this weekend. I tried to ask you yesterday, but I never got a chance."

"You're going to be gone?" I couldn't help sounding disappointed.

"Yeah, my mom's going to meet a client in Springfield, and she's taking me with her. Says when she's not working, she's going to take me shopping."

"You're skipping school for two days to go shopping?" I asked incredulously.

"Against my will, but yes. Apparently, my wardrobe needs revamping."

"Why can't she just leave you at home, and just buy things in your size? I mean, guys don't really have to try things on like girls do."

"Well, I'm also kind of getting fitted for a tuxedo, and I have to be there for that."

"You're renting a tux in Springfield? For the dance?"

"Actually, mom's buying me a tux. Say's it's a good investment."

"I'm so jealous. I wish I could go shopping. I'm borrowing a dress from Carrie, and I won't even see it until Saturday, so hopefully it fits," I admitted.

"I'm sure you'll look amazing no matter what you're wearing."

I blushed, and was glad that Justin couldn't see it. "Sure, yes, I'll get your work for you."

"Good, I was hoping I could come by your place and get it sometime Saturday afternoon."

"Sorry, but I'm going to be at Carrie's all day Saturday."

"You've been spending a lot of time with Carrie and Brittany lately. Which reminds me, how was Tuesday night?" Justin asked.

210

"It was fun. It's surprising, but we have a lot in common."

"So, how about Sunday morning?"

"For what?"

"Can I come by Sunday morning and get my homework?"

"Yeah, that will be fine."

"Well, I should let you go. Think of me while you're in class."

I could tell he was teasing, but I knew I would.

☐

Knowing that Justin wouldn't be there was actually nice. I wasn't nervous about how I should act or what I should say, and I didn't spend my time watching for him. Plus, I wanted to have the whole mind control thing under control when I saw him. I needed to be sure that I wouldn't make him strip off his shirt, just because I happen to remember how much I liked seeing his chest, or anything else like that. So, I decided to spend the next couple of days practicing.

The good news was that it turned out to be easier than it had been when I was still blocked. The bad news was that it turned out to be easier. I no longer needed to shout or push so forcefully with my mind, in order to get results. I learned that the hard way. I tried to make Jason Esposito place his math book on the floor in the hall. Something harmless, I thought, until fifty kids in the hall all dropped their books on the floor at the same time. Jason placed his on the floor real gently like I had wanted. Others weren't so gentle. Some went so far as to throw their books, hitting other people in the process, and one boy, standing not far from where I was, actually fell down himself. I think I literally knocked him over with my mind; either that or it was a very strange coincidence.

Afterward everyone was looking around, like, "That was weird", and then people started laughing about it, or horsing around. I heard one Goth boy take credit for it, and threaten another kid that next time he'd do something worse. I was happy to just slink away to class. I was going to have to do better.

After that, I tried being more subtle. When I was getting dressed for PE, I told Darla Parker to wear a side ponytail. I know, it's a weird thing to make someone do, but I was going for harmless, and I couldn't think of anyway a ponytail could hurt anyone.

So, while I was seemingly absorbed with putting on my gym shoes, I sent the thought to Darla, who was at the locker next to me. I barely even thought the command, but every girl in my PE class came out of that locker room wearing a side ponytail—even me, since I didn't want to do anything to make me stand out. The strange thing was that it seemed to catch on. Later that day, girls I'd never met were running around looking like they'd just stepped out of the 80s, minus the big bangs and leg warmers.

At lunch, I told Carrie and Brittany what I had been doing, and Brittany, who was either very brave or very trusting, let me practice on her. After a couple of failed attempts to have *only* Brittany tap her fingers of the table, Brittany suggested I try addressing her by name in my head, before sending her any subliminal messages, and it worked. Then, just to be sure, I made her meow like a cat, quack like a duck, and moo like a cow. I would have done more, but by that point she'd had enough.

The rest of the day went more smoothly. I made Mrs. Howitzer, my algebra teacher, pick her nose. I made Mr. Conway, the principal, pick out a wedgie. And I made Mrs. Tooney, my English teacher, say "I love pork rinds" when the bell rang. But just so you know, it wasn't only teachers that I picked on. I made people all around me drop pencils, trip on imaginary objects, spill their milk, hum to themselves, and anything else I could think of.

By the end of the day, several people had noticed that something weird was going on, but, luckily, none of it could be linked to me. Most people blamed it on the full moon. Only Carrie, Brittany, and myself knew the truth.

That night, as I watched TV, I couldn't help thinking about the day, and all the things I'd done, and I felt kind of bad. I hated my gift. The things I'd done weren't terrible, but they hadn't been nice either. The truth was I couldn't think of any way my power could ever be good. It is mind control after all, and, truthfully, I never wanted to use it again.

Unfortunately, I would need more practice in order to do that. I would have to use my power in order to learn how to *not* use it, but I was determined that I would try to find good ways to use it from now on.

On Friday, I arrived at school hopeful. I was only going to do good things, but I quickly became discouraged. There just wasn't any possible way that mind control could be good. But I still needed practice. I was about to give up, and go back to doing not so nice things, when I saw a girl throw a gum wrapper in the grass near the door to the art room.

In a split-second decision, I made her pick it up and throw it away. I was smiling as I entered the art room. I'd stopped her from littering. I'd done something good.

After that, I saw things all around me. I made boys open doors for girls. I made people say "please" and "thank you", I made people recycle their cans at lunch, and I made people talk respectfully to their teachers. By the end of the day, I'd had no accidents, and I'd gotten the practice I'd needed. I felt confident that I could shield my ordinary thoughts from being broadcasted to those around me, and that I could control people if I wanted to. More importantly, I felt confident that I could avoid controlling others when I wasn't meaning to.

When I got home from school, I was exhausted. It had taken a lot out of me to not influence everyone. I trudged through the rest of my afternoon responsibilities: laundry, dishes, dinner, etc.—all those things I'd never had to worry about while my mom was around, but that now fell on my shoulders because there was no one else to do them. When I finished washing the last dish I'd used at dinner, and I realized that everything was done, I rushed to my room and slipped beneath the covers. The sun had barely set, but I was asleep within minutes.

The next day was the dance, and I fell asleep thinking about Justin, and wondering if every day would be as exhausting as that one had been.

☐

The dream started out normal, well, as normal as dreams can be. I was sitting in Mr. Pruitt's biology class, when suddenly I was the only person in the room and I realized that it was Saturday. I was getting up to go home when a cat walked in and told me it was time to go. When I got to the hall, I realized that Justin was my ride, and I started chasing him down the hall but he was always just out of my reach. I followed him out the door and suddenly we're both standing on a high cliff over a roiling ocean. He turned to me and smiled, then very casually stepped over the edge. I screamed and reached for him, and fell over myself. As I was falling to my death, I began looking around for Justin and found him hovering right beside me. Growing out of his back were two of the biggest most beautiful wings I'd ever seen, which was great for him, but didn't help me at all. Terrified I looked down at the rapidly approaching jagged rocks below me, and I screamed.

"Don't worry," Justin said calmly. "You won't crash."

"How do you know?" I asked.

"Because you have wings too," he said.

I looked over my shoulder, and he was right. My wings expanded at just the right moment and I glided safely above the surface of the water before flying back toward Justin.

219

"Thank you," I said, reaching my hand out to his.

Just before he took my hand, the necklace around my neck—my mother's necklace—became white hot and began burning a hole through my chest.

☐

I woke with a jerk, frantically feeling my chest and back. I was okay, but my leg was killing me. I stuck my hand into the pocket of my jeans and pulled out my mom's necklace. I had been carrying it with me ever since I took it out of that box, though I still couldn't bring myself to put it on. I had been laying on it.

I rubbed the indention in my leg and looked at the clock. It was already nine o'clock. I was supposed to be at Carrie's in an hour, and considering that I didn't know exactly where she lived I knew I needed to hurry.

After showering and getting dressed, I got in my car and headed east of town on Highway 32, following the directions Carrie had given me. At five till ten, I pulled up outside Carrie's house and gasped.

It was huge.

I parked in the circle drive behind Brittany's red Mazda, and headed for the front door. Carrie, who was still in her pajamas, answered on the second knock, clearly expecting me.

As Carrie took my arm and led me upstairs, I took in the vaulted ceilings and marble floors. "What does your mom do?"

"She makes movie trailers," Carrie shrugged.

"Really? Have I seen any of hers?" I asked, truly surprised.

"You know that romantic comedy that just opened this weekend? It's her latest one, but she's always working on something."

"Why does she live here? Why not in Hollywood?"

"She likes it here, and plus it's Hollywood after all."

"What do you mean?" I asked, confused.

"The Graces. Hollywood is full of them, and my mom doesn't want to be associated with them."

I really didn't understand the feud between Sirens and Graces but I decided to drop it.

We arrived at Carrie's Cinderella bedroom where Brittany was lounging in a big overstuffed chair wearing a burgundy satin robe.

"Hey," Brittany said, barely glancing up from the gossip magazine she was reading.

"Let me get a robe for you," Carrie said, heading for her huge walk in closet.

"What are we going to do for nine hours?" I asked Brittany, quietly.

"Spa treatments, of course," Brittany said.

"Is that safe? I mean, it's only been a few days…"

"For *you*. It's been a little bit longer for *us*," Brittany said, finally looking up from her magazine.

"Which is why you will be getting a massage and a lot of good conversation, while Brittany and I get the celebrity treatment," Carrie said, coming out of her closet with a navy-blue silk robe draped over her arm.

My eyebrows went up. "Really?"

"You better go get changed. Jeanie, my massage therapist, will be here in about twenty minutes to give each of us massages," Carrie said.

223

I took the robe and headed for her bathroom

"Today is all about girl time. Every girl needs it," Carrie added, "especially us."

Brittany looked at me and rolled her eyes, but her smile betrayed her.

"Sounds like fun," I said to Carrie.

"Tonight, is going to be fun. Today is going to be awesome," Carrie said.

Chapter 18

Several hours later, I stood examining myself in the mirrors. (There were three of them, like in the dressing room of a store.) Carrie had a closet full of dresses, some with the tags still on, and I had tried on most of them. In the end, I had chosen a white baby doll dress. The top was sleeveless and form fitting, and just below the bust line hung several layers of semitransparent white gauze with silver threads woven through it that hung to just above my knees.

My hair was up in a simple French twist, and for shoes, I'd chosen white summer sandals. My make up was simple but flawless. It was near freezing outside, and I looked like I was ready for a moonlit stroll on the beach. What was I thinking?

You were thinking about him…

I was. I was thinking about Justin and summer.

Justin was always somewhere in the periphery of my mind, whether I was thinking about him or not. But thinking his name, had brought him to the foreground of my thoughts, and once again, I thought I could almost feel him. As if we were tied together by an invisible thread, and his every move tugged on that thread. The tugs weren't very strong—as if he were far away, and they had to travel a long distance—but I could still feel them pulling me toward him, wherever he was.

I closed my eyes, hoping I'd see him, but found only darkness.

I opened my eyes. Those visions had probably only been my imagination anyway.

"You going with the white one?" Brittany asked coming up behind me wearing a black spandex cocktail dress with a halter-top. Her long black hair flowed freely down her back.

"Looks like it," I said, still watching my own reflection.

"I still think you should wear the red one," Brittany said adjusting her boobs and turning to look at her profile. "The red one looked hot. In the red one you looked like you were out to steal you a man."

"You look like a goddess," I told her, catching her eye in the mirror.

"I know, don't I?" Brittany said, flashing her alluring smile at herself.

"And just so you know, I'm going to steal my man, even in this dress."

Brittany's eyes met mine approvingly, and a conspiratorial smile curled her red lips. "I guess it doesn't matter if we look like a devil or an angel, underneath we're Sirens and we'll get our man either way."

"So, which man will *you* be getting tonight, Aaron or Chris?" I asked, shifting the conversation away from me.

"I couldn't decide so…" Brittany smiled mischievously.

"So…what?"

"So, I'm going with both of them."

I smiled despite myself, and nudged Brittany with my hip. "You are so bad."

"What has she done now?" asked Carrie, as she emerged from her closet. She wore a floor length, midnight blue dress. Her mane of blonde curls was swept up into some sort of bun in the back. A jeweled diadem rested high on her forehead and disappeared into her hair. She looked like a queen.

While I could imagine hunky bare-chested servants feeding grapes to Brittany as she lounged in her temple, the sight of Carrie brought images of knights and commoners alike bowing down to her, serving her with devotion, dying for her honor.

"Nothing much," Brittany said. "I've simply invited another guest to our party."

"Meaning?" Carrie asked.

"I have two dates tonight, so I hope there's room in the limo for one more," Brittany said.

I still couldn't believe how brazen Brittany was. Both Aaron and Chris were high profile seniors. They weren't my type, but I was impressed nonetheless.

"And you approve of this?" Carrie said, turning on me.

I sobered a little. "You have to admit it's impressive."

Carrie obviously wanted to say something but she stopped herself. Then tersely she checked her appearance in the mirror once more and stalked out of the room.

"What was that about?" I asked.

"I don't know," Brittany said shrugging. "I'm forever disappointing her, but she did seem pretty upset, even for her. Whatever, she'll get over it."

"I thought you two were best friends," I said.

"We are, but that doesn't mean we agree on everything," Brittany said. Then eying me added, "But maybe I've found someone to have my kind of fun with."

I laughed. "Brittany, I don't judge you for the things you do, but that doesn't mean I plan on joining you. I'm more of a one-man kind of girl."

"And after tonight he'll be all yours," Brittany said, unoffended.

A shiver of excitement ran through me. I may not have looked like royalty or deity, but based on my appearance alone, I couldn't imagine not getting any man I wanted. Janie wouldn't have a chance.

☐

When the limousine pulled into the parking lot of the church where the dance was being held, I was surprised to see my white Neon among the cars parked there, and I mentioned it to Carrie.

"I had everyone's cars brought here. I didn't think you all would want to have to come back to my house to get them," Carrie said. Then with a withering glance at Brittany, who was sitting at the other end of the limo flanked by her dates, she added, "Besides, some of you may have plans after the dance."

Though Brittany's dates were both vying for her attention, she met my eyes and winked.

231

I couldn't help the blush that reddened my face. I honestly hadn't thought about that part of her date, and really didn't want to.

"Well, thanks," I said to Carrie.

"No problem," she said, giving me a genuine smile before turning her attention back to Dustin, her date. At school, he wasn't the most popular boy, he was too artsy for that, but at that moment he looked like a knight, poised and ready to slay dragons for his queen.

Carrie had forgiven me for earlier, but I wasn't sure I had forgiven her yet. Though I hadn't shown it, it had irritated me that she assumed I would do something like bring two dates to a dance. I wasn't going to judge Brittany for doing it. To her it didn't matter which guy she was with, and if she wanted to just have fun that was her choice.

With Carrie and Brittany occupied, I turned to my date. From the moment, he had arrived, Collin had been nothing but a gentleman—giving me compliments, opening doors—it almost made me feel bad for inviting him under false pretenses. He had always been nice to me, and I had to admit that he looked nice in his rented tux, but at that moment he looked uncomfortable.

"Thanks for the flowers," I said, giving Collin a friendly smile. "They're beautiful."

Collin seemed to relax a little. "They pale in comparison to you."

I felt a blush creeping back into my cheeks, and I turned away smiling. Boys had been complimenting me a lot lately, but there was something about the way Collin was looking at me that made his seem more genuine.

As we got out of the limo and headed for the door, I tried to push the conversation back into a *just friends* category. I didn't want to lead him on. "So, what are you going to do for your big end of the semester project in biology?"

"I'm not sure, but I was thinking about a study of people and relationships."

"What kind of study?"

"I was thinking maybe following a handful of couples, recording how their relationships progressed, getting the male verses the female perspective," Collin said.

"That sounds interesting. You don't happen to be in Psychology, do you?"

"Actually, I was hoping I could use the case study for both classes," Collin admitted.

"Who do you have for Psychology?"

"Mrs. LeMont."

"Oo, I've heard she's tough," I said.

"She's strict, but I'm learning a lot. What are you planning on doing for your biology project?"

"I'm watching a tree, observing how it changes through the seasons."

"Sounds exciting," Collin said sarcastically.

We had arrived at the door, and Collin opened it to let me in.

Just inside the door was a table with a sign that said, 'Pay Here'. Beyond that was a set of double doors that led into the church's cultural hall. I could hear loud talking and the bass of whatever song was playing.

We got in line to pay.

Justin was somewhere beyond those doors; I could feel him. I took a deep breath and instinctively felt for my pocket, but my hand found only the gauzy material of my dress. I'd left the necklace at home. My newfound confidence faltered.

Collin handed the woman at the table some cash.

What if, even as a Siren, he doesn't want me? What if Janie looks better than me? What if I make a fool of myself?

No, I am a Siren. And I have other abilities besides just beauty...

I didn't want to think about that. I wasn't going to use mind control to make Justin want me. I just couldn't do that.

"Are you ready?" Collin asked, walking with me into the cultural hall.

I nodded. Brittany, Carrie and their dates had joined the line behind me. I had hoped that we'd all stick together as a group or something, but it looked like they'd abandoned me for their dates. I wouldn't have minded, except that I was about to abandon my date too, and I felt bad for him.

Why did they talk me into bringing a date? I should have come alone. Maybe I should dance with him once, just to be nice.

I wasn't sure what the theme for the dance was, but in the middle of the dance floor, a fountain glowed a deep magenta, while cardboard silver stars hung from the ceiling among cut out puffy clouds in various shades of pinks and purples. It was like stepping into a sunset.

"Would you like to dance," Collin asked.

The dance floor was crowded, and as we danced, I couldn't help scanning the crowd for Justin.

"He's over there," Collin said, startling me.

"What? Who?" I asked innocently.

"Justin Smith."

"Why would you assume…" I stammered.

"Look, I've seen you two together. I thought you guys had something going on."

"Our relationship is complicated," I said, looking at his slicked hair, the collar of his shirt, anywhere but his face.

"Is that complication named Janie, by any chance?"

I couldn't look at him.

"Look, don't get upset. I figured you only asked me out to make him jealous or something."

"Then why did you come?"

"I was flattered," Collin said, and shrugged. "It's not every day that a beautiful girl asks me out."

"I'm sorry. Just so you know I really do enjoy your company, which is why I asked you."

"I wish you would have been straightforward with me."

We danced in silence for a few minutes.

238

"You must hate me right now," I whispered.

"I'm alright," Collin said, catching me eye. "Really, no offense, but I never thought of you as more than a friend anyway."

"I'd like that," I said, "to be your friend."

"Then friends it is," Collin said, attempting to twirled me, but stepping on my foot in the process.

"Sorry."

"No, it's okay. You're not so bad," I said, trying to be kind. I still hadn't gotten the nerve to look in the direction Collin had said Justin was, and I was stalling.

"You want to make him jealous? Well, now's your chance. He's staring right at us."

I couldn't resist any longer and I chanced a look over my shoulder.

Justin was standing on the other side of the room with a small group of people. He was wearing a solid black, tailor-made tuxedo. His pale skin stood out in contrast to his dark features, making him look devastatingly handsome. Janie was at his side, wearing a backless red dress. She looked amazing, but Justin was looking at me.

I felt an urge to run to him, but resisted it.

"I could kiss you," Collin said, interrupting my thoughts.

"What?"

"You want to make him jealous or not?"

"Collin, I'm not going to kiss you," I said as gently as possible.

"It was worth a shot. I'm not sure it's necessary anyway. If looks could kill, you'd be dancing with a corpse."

"That's a pleasant image," I laughed.

"It's what I do," Collin said, smiling at me.

"Why are you helping me?" I asked, sobering.

Collin met my eyes. "That's what friends do."

"Then I'm lucky to have a friend like you," I said.

The song ended.

"I think I'm going to get some punch," Collin said backing away.

"Do you want me to come?" I asked awkwardly, unsure what I should do.

"No, you have a visitor anyway," Collin said. "I'll see you at school."

"Collin…"

"It's alright," he said and walked away.

"Where's he off to?" Justin asked behind me.

"I think he's going home," I said, sorry to have used Collin, but happy he had taken it so well.

"Only a fool would leave you," Justin said.

This is it.

I turned around and looked up into his dark eyes, my heart racing.

"Would you like to dance?" Justin asked.

"What about your date?" I asked, tearing my eyes away from Justin's to find Janie watching us.

"She knows that I promised you a dance."

Our bodies were mere inches apart, not yet touching, and the pull of him was nearly unbearable.

"One dance?" I asked. *What if I don't give you back?*

Justin held my gaze, then placed his hand on my lower back, drawing me to him. His touch sent electricity coursing through my body, awakening a need inside of me that I'd never felt before. I'd never been alive until that moment.

"Do you know how beautiful you are?" Justin whispered, his lips brushing my ear, sending a pleasant shiver down my spine.

I lifted my head from his shoulder and looked up at him, catching my breath. In his eyes I saw the same desire I was feeling. I wanted him to kiss me.

Then his hands were on my neck, his thumbs caressing my jaw line, and he brought his lips to mine.

The moment our lips touched the rest of the world disappeared. We were the only beings in existence and the only things that mattered were his lips on mine, his hands in my hair. I felt excited and peaceful at the same time, like I'd been lost all of my life and I'd finally come home.

When he drew away, he took the sunlight and the universe with him. Justin settled his arms around my waist, and looked at me, watching for my reaction.

"Winter, I love you," Justin said.

My heart fluttered. I felt stronger, though my legs felt weak. I had waited so long for this moment, for Justin to look at me the way he was watching me, for him to say he loved me.

I love you too, I thought.

I did love him. I loved him with every fiber of my being, with all of my soul. I'd been in love with Justin since I was nine, but I'd never felt anything as strong as I felt at that moment.

The first kiss, though sincere, had been simple, innocent. A question. The second one carried with it all of the love and emotion the first kiss had only hinted at. I was acutely aware of my body pressed against Justin's, the pounding of my heart, the fluttering of my stomach, his hands on my back, the silky feel of his hair between my fingers.

My thoughts were a whirlwind of emotions. *Happy.*

Nervous. Excited. Scared. Happy. Anxious. Happy. Happy.

He loves me. He needs me.

It's not real…

The thought was like being doused with cold water. The excitement faded.

Abruptly, I pull away from his kiss, holding onto his shoulders for support. Then I stepped out of his embrace.

I love him. That is real.

If I really love him, I can't do this to him. I won't take away his will.

"Winter, if I'm going too fast…" Justin said, his unfinished sentence lingering in the air between us.

I love you. I need you. You make me whole, complete. I've loved you my whole life, and because I love you, because I really, deeply love you, I can't do this.

Silently, I thought all the things I wanted to say, but couldn't. Aloud, I said, "Justin, I…"

My throat closed, stopping the words I had to say. Stalling, I looked around, drawing courage for what I was about to do.

We had danced ourselves to a secluded corner of the room. The light from the fountain was alternating colors in time with the music, and other couples were separating as the song changed to a fast dance. I saw Janie searching the dance floor for us, clearly upset. I felt sorry for her and envied her at the same time. Her date had abandoned her, but he would soon be returning.

"Justin, you need to go back to Janie," I finally said, unable to look at him.

Justin tilted my face to his, searching my eyes.

"Winter."

My name was like a breath, a plea, on his lips. It would be so easy to step back into his strong arms and lose myself in him again.

"Justin, we can't. I want you to go back to your date," I said, desperately holding back the rush of tears that were threatening.

Justin drew me back to him, circling me in his arms, and the ache for him eased a little.

"I don't believe you," Justin said into my hair.

Pressed against him, with his arms around me, the world was right again. I closed my eyes drinking it in. It would be the last time my world would ever be right.

Justin, I love you.

Then I mustered all of my strength, and stepped away from him.

"Justin, this can't happen. Please don't follow me," I said. Then I turned and ran out the door.

Chapter 19

The phone was ringing again, but I made no effort to answer it. The answering machine had filled up a long time ago, and now the phone just continued to ring. I should have turned off the ringer.

Maybe I will, I thought, but made no effort to do that either. He would eventually hang up.

It was Sunday afternoon, and I was curled up in a ball on my couch watching nothing in particular on the TV with the volume turned down. My hair still showed some semblance of a French twist, but most of it had fallen down, and I'm sure my makeup was smeared from crying, but I hadn't checked. I had at least changed into some sweats. Carrie's dress lay balled up on the floor.

I pulled my knees closer and wished the phone would stop. Twenty rings later it did.

I had set the homework I'd gotten for Justin outside my apartment door before the sun was even up, and then fallen asleep on the couch. Justin had come hours ago to get it. He had pounded on the door for what seemed like forever, calling my name, begging me to talk to him, but eventually he had given up, or so I thought. That was when the phone started ringing. And ringing. And ringing.

How was I going to do this? I couldn't hide in my apartment forever. I had to go to school. I hadn't planned for this part of my decision. I hadn't expected him to act like this. I'd hoped he would accept my decision and leave me to suffer in silence.

What have I done?

I was tempted to just move somewhere else, somewhere far away, somewhere where I could disappear. But I hadn't moved here for Justin. I'd moved here for my mom, and I couldn't just uproot her because I had messed up, because I was a coward.

No, I would just have to be strong. Eventually he would understand that I meant what I'd said—that we couldn't be together. Until then... I'd never intentionally used my powers of persuasion on him, but I would if I had to.

I hugged my knees tighter. *I can do this. I have to do this.*

Thinking it, I did feel a little stronger. Then the knocking on my door started again, and my conviction faltered.

Justin was so close. It would be so easy to just open the door and let him into my home, into my life. I could have everything I wanted. He would love me and want me, and I would love him. We could be so happy.

But even as I thought it, I knew it wasn't true. Every look, every touch, every kiss would be painful. Yes, he thought he loved me, but it wasn't real, and how long would it be before he realized that as well. How long would it be before it was *him* leaving *me*? I couldn't handle that.

No, as hard as this was going to be, it was better than the alternative. If I gave him my heart, gave him everything I was, and he left me, I wouldn't survive.

I could get my tubes tied.

The thought was my heart's last attempt to justify giving in, but I knew it was wrong. For some reason, I didn't think it would work. If that's all it took, I was sure I wouldn't even be alive.

The knocking came again.

Suddenly, the stress of the day and the previous night, the frustration of my situation, and anger at Justin for putting me through this overwhelmed me, and I swung the door open.

"Collin," I said, shocked.

"Winter?" Collin said, sounding concerned.

My eyes welled up, and a sob escaped my throat. It was better that it wasn't Justin, I told myself.

Suddenly Collin was guiding me to my couch, his arm around me.

"Winter, did he hurt you?" Collin asked with restrained anger.

I was disheveled and sobbing. It only took a minute to realize what he must be thinking.

"What? NO!" I said, regaining some of my composure.

"Oh." Collin let out a held breath. "I thought he was interested. I'm sorry, I should have stayed."

"Hee iss intarressbed," I said dissolving into new sobs.

"What?"

Collin handed me a tissue, and I wiped my face and caught my breath.

"He is," I said more clearly, blowing my nose.

"What? Interested?"

I nodded.

"But I thought…Then what's the…" Collin asked, grasping for some way to figure out what was wrong without prying or offending me.

"It's complicated," I said.

"Is there anything I can do?"

I looked over at him, my eyes finally clear. "Collin, why are you even here?"

Collin held out a silver chain with a diamond pendant. "I went to return my tux, and found this in my pocket."

"Carrie's necklace," I said.

The chain of the necklace had broken in the limo on the way to the dance, and Collin had put it in his pocket for safekeeping.

"Thank you, I'm sure she'll want it back," I said, taking it from his hand.

There was a moment of awkward silence.

"Well, I should probably go." Collin said.

"Yeah." I stood and walked him to the door.

"I'll see you tomorrow," Collin said, then added, "at school?"

"I'll see you at school," I assured him. "And, Collin, thank you."

Collin smiled shyly. "Yeah, see you."

Chapter 20

Collin smiled at me as I rushed into the biology room just as the tardy bell rang. I'd timed my arrival to school just right so as to avoid as many people as possible. Unfortunately, I couldn't avoid all of them. Doug something or other was sitting at my desk.

"Hey, Winter. I saw what happened at the dance Saturday. That's a bummer," Doug said as I stood awkwardly at my desk with nowhere else to go. He didn't sound like he thought it was a 'bummer'.

"Okay," I said.

"So, does that mean you're available this Saturday?"

"No."

"Well, if you change your mind, here's my number," Doug said, pulling out a pen. Then he snatched my notebook from my hands.

I grabbed my folder back but not before he had defaced it with his name and phone number. Then, much to my relief he left to go sit on his side of the room. I sat down in my vacated seat and turned around to see Collin smiling at me.

"What?" I asked, irritated.

"Nothing," Collin said, unfazed by my attitude.

"Would you happen to need a folder?" I asked, holding out the folder for Collin to see.

Collin laughed, which irritated me more. "No thanks."

"Class please be seated," Mr. Pruitt said from the front of the room.

"Fine," I said and turned back around.

"Don't you just love Mondays," Collin said behind me.

"Shut up," I muttered back. I wasn't sure when we had gotten to the point in our friendship where he enjoyed seeing me suffer, but clearly, we'd arrived.

About half way though class Derrick Pierce passed me a note that said he wanted to talk to me after class, and by the looks he was giving me, I was pretty sure why. Then I caught the tall boy next to me staring at me again. His name is Keith Fiekleman. (He introduced himself this time.) The day had barely started, and already I had three admirers. When class let out, I rushed out the door and right into Justin.

Justin's hands caught my elbows, and some of my stress eased. Touching Justin felt so natural, and for a moment I felt as though I'd just climbed under a warm down comforter on a rainy day, but then I pulled back and so did Justin, reluctantly.

"Winter, we need to talk," Justin said, his face a mask.

"Okay. Walk with me. I have to get to the other side of campus," I said.

Justin fell into step beside me, as he had done many times before. Neither of us said a word, and I had visions of us walking in companionable silence forever. But as much as I liked to believe that Justin was meant to be a part of my life, I knew it couldn't last. One or both of us would eventually try to bridge that gap between us, would try to draw the other closer, and I couldn't let that happen.

"Winter, I don't know what I did wrong, but I'd do anything to set it right," Justin finally said. "Kissing you felt right, and I'm not going to apologize for it. It was what you wanted too, I know it was. Even now I don't think you want this barrier between us, but you're throwing it up anyway, and I don't understand why. If I moved too fast, then tell me, but don't shut me out completely. I need you," Justin said.

259

I wished things could be different. I wished I could fall into his arms again. Out loud I said, "Can't we just go back to the way it was? Back before boy/girl stuff complicated things?"

"You mean back when you were rude and I threw clumps of dirt in you hair?" Justin smiled at the memory.

Back before I knew what I was. Before it changed things. I can't have a relationship with you. I can't have a relationship with anyone. "Yeah, something like that."

We'd stopped walking now and Justin reached over and pulled a loose piece of my hair behind my ear. "If that is what you really want," Justin said, and very gently whispered my name.

I couldn't have him touching me like this, I was losing focus.

"I have to go to class," I said, pulling myself out of my dreamlike thoughts. "Goodbye," I said, before I left Justin standing alone in the hall by the entrance to the gym. It sounded very final, and it was meant to.

Gym class sucked, but no surprise there. Ultimate Frisbee is not for the uncoordinated, and honestly, I think there should be some kind of alternative activity offered for those of us who can't run and catch things at the same time—like taking a nice slow walk or something. Coach Reid seemed to have gotten control of himself, which I was happy about, even if being able to sit out again would have been nice. The rest of the class was girls, and while they didn't look like they were too happy with me, at least no one ambushed me and asked me out. Even so, I was happy to go to Art when the bell rang.

There is something about the smell of art supplies, the scratch of pencil on paper that can make me forget everything else. Art has always been my haven, the place where I could disappear for a while into my own little world, as I try to create something. I needed an escape, a break from this wreck of a day, but I wouldn't get it.

The moment I walked into Mrs. Rosie's room I recognized the problem. There were five boys in my art class. One of them was Derrick Pierce. I'd managed to avoid him in Biology, where there were rules about getting out of your chair and talking, but Art is different. In Mrs. Rosie's class, we were allowed to get up and talk as long we got our work done, and Derrick was waiting for me.

"Hey Winter," Derrick said as I entered the room, and four other pairs of eyes turned to watch.

"Hey, Derrick," I said with no enthusiasm. He didn't seem to notice.

"I tried to catch you after Biology, but you seemed busy with Justin. I thought that's okay, I can wait. How is Smith?" Derrick asked.

Derrick was on the football team, just barely, but that didn't stop him from having the attitude that he was God's gift to women.

"He's good," I said, trying to contain my annoyance.

I sat down between two other girls and began taking out my art supplies, hoping he would get the hint and go to his seat. He didn't. Instead, he turned to Sarah Hopkins, the girl on my left, and flashed her his perfect toothpaste ad smile.

"You don't mind if I sit here, do you?" he asked her, each word dripping with syrup.

Sarah of course got all shy with a big silly grin and said, "No, of course not." Then she picked up her stuff and found another seat.

I was stuck with him.

"So, next weekend my parents are going out of town, and I was hoping you could come over and keep me company," Derrick said.

"No thank you," I said through clenched teeth.

"Oh, come on, Baby, don't be like that," Derrick said, and placed a hand on my leg for emphasis.

That was about the time I snapped. I didn't care whether it was ethical or not, I wanted him to go away.

Derrick, you need to go to the bathroom, and when you come back you will sit in your normal seat.

I felt the thought skip through the air between us. Then his eyes glazed over a little before he got up and asked Mrs. Rosie if he could go to the bathroom.

I'd done it, even though I'd promised myself I wouldn't, and I didn't feel bad about it. I wasn't sure what that meant.

Then I noticed the empty seat beside me and sent out a thought to everyone in the room to leave me alone. This strange new power of mine was impressive and a little scary. I kept thinking about Uncle Ben's words of wisdom to Peter Parker about how power comes with responsibility. I wasn't sure I was responsible enough to wield such power. But I was using it anyway.

It worked, and all too soon the bell was ringing and it was time for Spanish. Luckily, most of the boys in that class were underclassmen and seemed too nervous to approach me.

265

Then it was lunchtime, and I was scanning the seats in the cafeteria, with butterflies in my stomach. It felt like the first day of school all over again. I wasn't sure where to go. It was raining outside so the outdoor table where Brittany and Carrie usually sat was vacant. When I found them, the butterflies in my stomach turned to worms. They were sitting next to Justin, my Justin, and Janie was with them.

This is good. He needs to move on.

It didn't feel good.

I ignored the little wave Carrie gave me and headed for Amanda's table. I hadn't really talked to her much lately, but I hoped she would still let me sit with her.

I put my tray of food down and began to sit when a high pitched, almost childlike voice said, "Decided to come and mingle with us lowly commoners?"

Sitting next to Amanda was Stacy White. She used to sit *near* me and Amanda, but had never really sat *with* us. She was petite with mousy brown hair, and I'd always imagined she would be sweet. It seemed I was wrong.

"Excuse me?" I asked.

"Slumming it today?" Stacy asked.

"I don't know what you mean."

"What I mean is, I don't know what happened between you and the other royal bitches, but we won't be your fall back friends, so leave."

Shocked, I looked at Amanda, who looked as though she wanted to say something, but then she just looked down and remained silent.

I was tempted to work my magic again, but instead I got up, dumped my uneaten food into the trash and walked out of the cafeteria. I'd lost my appetite anyway.

I was outside, the cold rain making my hair cling to my face and saturating my sweatshirt, when Collin found me.

"Hey," Collin said.

I nodded.

"It's frickin' cold out here," Collin said, sitting beside me on the wet bench.

"Collin, what do you want?" I was heart broken, lonely, and probably on the verge of getting sick from sitting in the rain. My patience was wearing thin.

Collin glared at me like he was going to tell me off, which I probably deserved, but instead he said, "Come on."

Collin stood up and headed for the doors to the senior hall. He didn't pause and he didn't look back to see if I had followed. I could have let him go, but I found myself just a few steps behind him.

Chapter 21

"Where are we going?" I asked once we were out of the rain.

"To my secret lair so I can have you all to myself." Collin let out an evil laugh and I rolled my eyes. Then he said in a normal voice, "To the library, where do you think?" and kept walking.

"You're such a dork," I said, but caught up to him.

Collin smiled as if I'd just given him a big compliment. "Seriously, how do you know I'm not sneaking you off somewhere to have my way with you?"

"Because I trust you," I said quietly and honestly, and for some reason *that* seemed to upset him, but we'd arrived at the library so I let it drop.

The school library wasn't the dark, musty stacks room I'd envisioned, but was bright and open, with one entire wall made of windows.

I followed Collin past the check out desk and around the carousels of computers to a table sitting in a large alcove.

More windows behind the table showed the front of the campus being drenched, as the steady rainfall turned into a torrential downpour. To the right was a wall of bookcases, and to the left was the back of the circulation desk.

"So," I finally said, turning to Collin, "is this were you spend your lunch period?"

"Most days, though sometimes I'm in the chemistry room."

"I had wondered why I had never seen you at lunch."

"Yeah, I prefer to avoid the whole lunchroom hierarchy," Collin said.

"I think I'd like to start. I've been at this school for two months now and I still don't know where I'm supposed to sit. Everyday it changes."

"Where do you want to sit?" Collin asked.

I thought about it for a second, playing with a loose thread on my jacket. "I used to know, but I'm not so sure anymore. Anyway, what we want isn't always what's best for us."

"Oh, well, I just wanted to know if you wanted to sit by the windows or by the books," Collin said sheepishly.

I looked down at the table with its empty plastic seats and blushed. I sat by the books.

"Just kidding."

I gasped, and swatted Collin's arm. "Butt hole."

Collin smiled, his green eyes sparkling. "So, do you want to talk about it?"

"What?"

"You know, the whole gloom and doom, sitting alone in the rain thing you've got going on."

"Oh, that," I said, laughing at myself, "Not really."

"Okay, so talk about something else."

"Like what?"

"Like what's your favorite color?"

"I don't know, blue, I guess. What's yours?"

"No, no, no. This is a get to know Winter game."

"So, I don't get to know Collin?"

"All in good time."

"Fine," I said, rolling my eyes, but I was smiling.

"Where was your favorite place you've lived? If the rumors are right, you've lived all over."

"Probably Rapid City. There is something about the Black Hills that's almost magical, but I could do without the horrible winters."

"What was your most embarrassing moment?" Collin asked.

I smiled and made a face. "Really? Fine." I took a deep breath. "I was nine and a friend of mine walked in on me while I was practicing kissing."

"Wait, what were you practicing on?"

"My hand, while I looked in the mirror. He, my friend, never said anything to me about it, but somehow that was almost worse. I kept waiting, expecting him to bring it up and humiliate me again, but he never did."

"Sounds like a good friend."

"He was," I said, smiling sadly.

"Of course, I probably would have made your life miserable until you begged for mercy," Collin admitted.

"Well, I'm glad it wasn't you who walked in on me," I said.

Collin smiled wickedly, "Then I would have kissed you to show you how it's done."

"Sure, you would have," I said sarcastically.

"What, you don't believe me?" Collin asked, leaning closer, reminding me a little too much of every other boy I'd talked to that day.

I sat back, trying not to look uncomfortable. Collin sat back too, and I relaxed.

"So, tell me about yourself, whatever you want to tell me," Collin said, his green eye probing, sincere.

I told him about my eccentric mother, about moving around so much, about my mother's accident, moving to

274

Salem. It was refreshing to talk to someone I had no history with, and who held no expectations. All too soon, the bell was ringing and lunch was over.

"Collin, could we do this again tomorrow?" I asked.

"Sure."

"Except tomorrow it's your turn under the microscope," I said, as we parted ways in the hall.

"Looking forward to it," Collin called over his shoulder.

I watched Collin walk away with disappointment. I liked Collin. While I was around him I was able to feel completely ordinary, but as all fairy tales must end, so had lunch and I was back to being Cinderella, the girl every boy had the hots for.

Algebra was the same old story. Andrew Jacobs sat a little too close to me, Nick Coleman kept asking me out, refusing to take no for an answer, and the rest of the boys in the class kept fawning all over me and trying to get things for me. At one point, I accidentally dropped my pencil and I was worried a fight was going to break out as three of them dived for it at once, but I snatched it up before they could get to it and saved them the trouble.

In American Government Matt Boli touched me. Doris had said that boundaries of etiquette usually stopped that sort of thing from happening. Lucky for me, either Matt was too weak to fight his urges or he didn't care much about boundaries, because right in the middle of class he reached over and began groping my arm. Yes, I said groping, and if you don't believe that an arm can be groped I'm here to tell you it can be. I was just glad that I hadn't been sitting close enough to him for him to reach any other part of my body.

After that, I'd had it. I mentally and physically told him to stop, and as soon as class was over I headed for the parking lot, but half way there I stopped. I couldn't hide forever. This wasn't some disease I was going to get over, it was my life now. I had to learn to deal with it, because I was going to have to deal with it every single day for the rest of my life. Resolutely, I turned back around and walked toward Mrs. Tooney's room for English.

As I sat down, Josh Hamilton turned in his chair and smiled at me. I smiled politely back, though it was getting harder and harder to do that. I had to keep reminding myself that I was irresistible to them, and they couldn't help it.

Josh, please just let me be.

I sent the thought out, sensing the now familiar static charge to the air as the thought passed from my mind to his. I didn't know what I'd do without my ability to do that. It seemed it was the only way I'd ever get any peace. I found

myself wondering how Carrie and Brittany dealt with this.

Chapter 22

"He groped you?" Carrie asked, stunned.

"Just my arm, but yes," I said into the phone.

After the day I'd had, I thought I wanted nothing more than to go home and get away from it all, except that once I was there the silence bothered me more. So, I'd called Carrie.

"So how do you deal with this? It seems the only thing I can do is control them, but there has got to be a better way."

Carrie laughed. "It gets better, though I've never had anyone actually touch me before."

"What do you think I should do?"

"Just keep being polite but firm. You are new and exciting right now. Eventually they will get used to you and won't bother you quite so much."

"How so? Will they build up a tolerance to me or something?" I asked incredulously.

"No, it's more like with practice they learn to control themselves better. But the desire never really goes away."

"Great."

"I missed you at lunch today," Carrie said.

"Sorry, I just couldn't sit over there with you guys, not with Justin there."

"Do you mind if I ask what happened between you two? I mean, you never really explained."

I sighed. "He kissed me."

"That's great, isn't it? That's what you wanted."

"I did. I wanted him to want me, except now I wish he wanted someone else," I began.

"Well, why don't you just make him do whatever you want then?" Carrie said.

"What?!"

"Why not, you do everyone else," Carrie added coolly.

I didn't know what to say. "Carrie, I though you of all people would understand."

"I understand perfectly. You know what, Winter, I've got to go. Just give my necklace to Brittany the next time you see her."

"Carrie, what...?" I started, but the line was already dead.

I stared at the phone then put it down. Collin had said he wouldn't be home tonight, and I was afraid to call Brittany. What if she suddenly turned on me as well? But the silence in my apartment was like a giant sitting on me. It spilled off the couch and flowed into the kitchenette, filling the empty spaces.

I pulled Boris closer, seeking whatever companionship I could, but he fought my advances and disappeared into the bedroom, leaving me alone.

I picked up the phone and dialed the first six digits of Justin's number before hanging up, and throwing the phone to the other end of the couch. I wouldn't.

Instead, I turned on the TV and the radio, filling my home with voices and noise, but it wasn't the same. I was all alone, and for the first time I really felt it.

Chapter 23

"So, why Justin?"

It was the next day, and I had just arrived at the library to find Collin waiting for me. The day had started out just as bad as the one before, maybe worse, and my first instinct was to just control everyone just to get some peace, but then I remembered what Carrie had said about me just controlling everyone, like I was some freaky dictator or something, and I restrained myself. I just put on a polite smile and suffered through it. The crazy thing was that a few months ago I probably would have loved to have the attention of every boy at school. I mean, it's like every dorky, unpopular girl's dream come true. I was suddenly the most popular, sought after girl in the school. At first, it had been fun and exciting, but there was never any down time. The boys' advances were like the winds of a storm that never let up, and I was just so tired of being driven by them. I would have given anything to be able to go back to sitting with Amanda, invisible to those around me. Because the truth was, I only ever wanted one person to really see me, and that dream was gone now.

"What do you mean, why Justin?" I asked, sitting down. In the back of my mind, I searched for Justin's presence, and found him far away somewhere. Probably off with Janie somewhere, I thought. I wasn't ready to talk about Justin.

"I mean, you move here. You keep to yourself, not talking to anyone," Collin said.

"I talked to people. I talked to you," I said a little defensively.

"About biology. I mean really talk to people. You don't let people in, and I get that, with the whole moving around thing, but why Justin? What was it about him that got you to lower your walls?"

Something inside of me recoiled. He was right. I didn't let people in. It had always been easier to keep people at a distance. It made things less complicated, and up until I'd lost my mother, it had been enough.

"I seemed to recall you agreeing to be put under the microscope today," I said, smiling, avoiding.

"It was the hair, wasn't it? That whole Clark Kent look just swept you off your feet?" Collin asked.

"You caught me. I'm a Superman fan, though if I had to choose I'd pick Tom Welling over Christopher Reeve every time."

"You watch Smallville?" Collin asked incredulously.

"Yes, but today's not about me. It's about you, sweety," I said, and pinched his cheek. It had worked. The conversation was back into safe territory.

"And you call me a dork," Collin muttered.

"As long as we're on the subject, what do you watch? Since Smallville is so far beneath you, and all."

"Dragon Ball Z…"

"You are giving me a hard time about Smallville, and you watch anime?"

"What's that supposed to mean?"

"It means anime sucks. I mean, don't the makers of all those cartoons realize that the drawing skills in our society have advanced beyond the mediocre stuff they are dishing out? It's like they intentionally hired art school flunkies."

"Cartoon? It's not a cartoon. It's Anime. And it's an art form of its own," Collin said defensively.

286

"Okay, I'm sorry. Let's just agree to disagree on TV, and find something else to talk about."

"Fine," Collin said, but I could tell he was still miffed.

I proceeded with caution. The last thing I needed was to tick him off.

"What's your favorite book?" I asked.

"Of Mice and Men," Collin said.

Steinbeck. Collin wasn't making this easy on me. I hated Steinbeck. He was always so dark and dreary. I had enough depressing things in my life, I didn't need to read about them as well. But I was determined not to offend my new friend.

"Really? Why's that," I asked genially.

"The characters are so real and believable," he said.

I could understand that. Some of my best friends were in the pages of books.

"What's your favorite food?"

"Italian."

Finally, something we agreed on. I loved Italian. We could build an entire relationship on Italian food alone.

"Favorite color?" I asked, feeling happier.

"Blue." Another plus.

"Most embarrassing moment?"

"No, I'm not answering that one," Collin said, looking uncomfortable.

"Oh, come on. I did," I said, smiling. "You have to."

"The dance," Collin muttered.

"What?" I hadn't heard him.

"The dance," Collin said, meeting my eyes before looking away, and I understood.

The dance. The dance where I ditched him for another guy. That dance.

"I'm sorry," I whispered.

"It's alright. I'm sorry. I shouldn't have mentioned it," Collin said taking my hand.

It was a friendly gesture, but it made me uncomfortable, and I pulled my hand back. I was afraid to ask anything else.

"Ask me what my favorite season is." Collin said.

I looked up through my lashes at him. "What's your favorite season?"

"Winter," Collin said.

I rolled my eyes but smiled.

The rest of the week went much the same way. I spent my days avoiding unwanted advances and my lunch period getting better acquainted with Collin. We had more in common then it originally seemed. He too was an only child, his father had left when he was just a baby, and his mother, though still conscious, had to work two jobs to support them, and was therefore gone most of the time. Because of this, he was involved in a lot of clubs, like Quiz Bowl, Drama Club, and National Honor Society, that kept him busy after school.

So, after school I would visit my mom for as long as I could, and when I wasn't with her I tried to keep busy doing homework and dishes and shopping for groceries. But I couldn't ignore the silence in my home or the lonely ache inside of me, no matter how hard I tried.

Justin was with me everywhere I went, hovering in the back of my mind, drawing me to him, but he kept his distance physically, giving me the space I'd asked for. And that just made me love him more. He was so good, and he deserved someone just as good. But that wasn't me. Controlling others came so naturally now, and what had once seemed appalling to me, wasn't looking so bad anymore. Yeah, I still tried to use my powers for good, but I did use them.

Carrie still wasn't talking to me, and Brittany wasn't so much as avoiding me as she was choosing to spend her time with Carrie. They had been friends longer, but it still hurt.

Before I knew it, it was Friday and the weekend was gaping open in front of me.

"So, what are you doing tonight?" I asked Collin.

We were in Biology, and in a minute Mr. Pruitt would begin his lecture.

"My mom got the weekend off so we can spend time together," Collin said.

"Oh," I said.

"I know it sounds really lame, but…"

"No, actually it sounds nice. What are you going to do?"

"I don't know. How about you?"

"I don't know."

Mr. Pruitt was starting class, and I had to turn around, but it was okay, because I didn't know what else to say. I wasn't looking forward to the weekend.

Later, at lunchtime, Collin and I had just sat down when two other boys walked over to our table in the library. One was tall with a buzz cut and built like a swimmer. The other was shorter with unruly dark hair and glasses.

"So, this is where you've been hiding," the tall one said.

The other one looked at me and smiled. "Hi. I'm Marc." He held out his hand to me, like he was going to shake it, but when I extended my own he gave it a kiss. Collin gave him a look and Marc dropped my hand.

"Winter, these boneheads are my friends Marc and Thomas. Marc and Thomas, meet Winter."

"She's hot, dude," Thomas said, and thumped Collin in the arm.

"Thanks. You know I can hear you, right?" I said, unleashing the full weight of my gaze at him.

Thomas reddened as if it hadn't occurred to him, and Marc snickered, as if Thomas's mistake would help his chances of getting me.

I smiled politely, like I'd been doing all week. The looks they were shooting at me were just as bad as Matt Boli. I closed my eyes and took a deep breath.

They are male, it's not their fault.

When I opened my eyes, and caught Collin watching me. It occurred to me again, how different he was than other boys. It wasn't as if he never flirted with me, or like he wasn't attracted to me. By now, I operated under the assumption that all boys were attracted to me, but there was something about the way he interacted with me that felt different than it did with other boys.

"Nice to meet you," I said politely, but I was uncomfortable. The library was my safe haven. Maybe that was what it was. Collin felt safe. For some reason, I trusted him to control himself around me. And it wasn't as if I didn't want to get to know his friends, it was just that they felt like every other boy at the school. Unpredictable.

Marc and Thomas sat down, and I glanced at the clock. Had it really only been five minutes. Lunch was going to last forever. I didn't know what to do. I could influence them, make them think they weren't attracted to me, but I didn't want to addle their brains unless it was necessary. Besides, it wasn't a permanent fix. The pull of the Siren would overpower the guise eventually.

I'd learned that my powers didn't really work in the long term. I couldn't really change ideas and opinions, not permanently. My influence was more like subliminal messages. I could suggest ideas and opinions for them, but as far as the future was concerned, I couldn't change their mind for them. But in the here and now, I had all control, if I wanted it. I could make them say or do anything I wished.

But we weren't to that point yet. They were Collin's friends, and I would show them the same courtesy I showed all of my friends. I wouldn't get inside their head unless I had to. In the meantime, I would just try to be as unappealing as possible, which meant not talking (because my voice had a magic of its own, even when I wasn't singing), not meeting their eyes, and generally trying to take up as little space in the universe as possible.

Across the table from me, Collin and his friends were arguing about what the plural form of the word penis should be. Collin thought should be penises, and Marc thought peni sounded better. But Thomas thought there should never be any circumstance where someone would have to be talking about penises in the plural form. Collin was right, but I kind of agreed with Thomas. Anyway, I wasn't about to add anything to that conversation, so I tried acting as invisible as possible, and searched in my mind for Justin.

Justin's presence in my mind was like a fire. If I mentally turned my back on it, and left it alone, it would die down to just glowing embers. But whenever I turned my attention to him, it would flare up like a huge bonfire, and fill me with a warmth that felt like his touch. The closer he was physically, the stronger the feeling. To my surprise, he wasn't in the cafeteria, or even on the school campus. Wherever he was, he was farther than the school grounds, and was getting farther away with every second.

He was in his car.

It made me sad that he was so far away. And the worst part was that I had no idea where he was going.

Chapter 24

"You back again?" the nurse with the big smile asked, as I entered the Nursing Home. I couldn't remember her name.

I gave her a weak smile. "Yeah. How is she?" I asked, signing in as a visitor.

After school, I'd gone straight to the nursing home, because I couldn't bear to be alone at the moment. I'd brought some CDs for my mom to listen to, because if she really was in there like everyone said, she was probably tired of the silence too.

"No change since yesterday, though I'm sure she loves the company," she said. Her name badge said Lila.

When I walked through the door to my mother's room, the first thing I noticed was the smell. Irises. Someone had left a large vase of purple and yellow irises on the table by her bed. I sat down the CDs I'd brought and returned to the receptionist's desk.

"Thank you for the flowers in my mom's room," I said, when Lila looked up at me.

"Wish I could take credit for them, but they're not from me."

"Then could you tell the nurse who put them there, thank you for me? Irises are my Mom's favorites."

"It wasn't from one of the nurses. They were from that boy who visited her earlier," Lila said, smiling.

"Boy?" As far as I knew, I had been my mother's only visitor since the day she had arrived in Salem, with the exception of the one visit from Doris.

"Hold on, let me find his name," Lila said, flipping through the visitor registry. "There he is. A Mr. Justin Smith."

Justin had given my mom flowers. Her favorite flowers.

"When was he here?" I asked, looking at my watch. I had left right after school and I'd just arrived. I couldn't imagine how he could have been there and gone already.

"Around lunchtime. Didn't you know? He's been coming and visiting her all week."

I thanked her, and returned to my mom's room. It was then that I saw the card sticking out of the flowers. It had my name on it.

Winter,

As you probably know by now, I've been visiting your mom. I hope you're not angry, but it just felt like the right thing to do. Besides, it's the closest I can get to spending my lunch period with you. Anyway, the irises are from my mom, but the other flower is for you.

Love,

Justin

I looked at the flower arrangement again. There hidden behind about a dozen irises was a single blue carnation. I picked it out and held it to my nose.

When I was eight, I decided that carnations were my favorite flower because they were the only flowers that could really be blue, because other 'blue' flowers were really just a shade of purple, and to me that was misleading and dishonest. I couldn't believe he had remembered.

For the next couple of hours, I played music for my mom, while I breathed in the scent of the carnation. It smelled like my childhood. When I was little my mom used to buy bouquets of carnations and we would make flower wreaths out of them. Then we would wear them on our heads like crowns and run around our house, or apartment, or wherever it was we

301

were living at the time, and pretend we were fairy princesses. I smiled at the still form of my mom lying next to me.

"You did a good job raising me, Mom. But I'm not grown yet. I still need you. Please come back to me."

My whispered plea hung in the air, but the only response was the constant beep of the heart monitor beside her, reminding me that at least she was still alive. And for that I was grateful.

When I left, it was just getting dark out, but I could already see several stars in the deep purple sky. My breath came out in little white clouds, and I rubbed my hands together to warm them up before taking hold of the cold steering wheel. The drive home was short enough that my car still hadn't warmed up by the time I was pulling into my parking space.

Once inside I just sat on my couch absorbing the heat until my numb fingers were red and stiff, and could grip a pencil again. Then I opened my backpack and pulled out my English book.

What? English? Where's my Math.

I looked inside my backpack, but there was no Algebra book to be found. I'd brought home the wrong book. I looked at the clock.

Six O'clock. There might still be someone at the school who could let me in. I grabbed my keys and ran out the door.

The school parking lot was deserted except for a dark SUV, a little Toyota, and my Neon. The lights were on in a few of the classrooms, but there was no response when I banged on the locked doors. After trying every available door and finding each locked, I gave up and returned to my car.

The lights in the parking lot hadn't come on yet, and I could barely make out the shapes of the Toyota and my Neon parked at the front of the lot. Lurking somewhere behind them in the shadows was the SUV. When I got a few feet from my car, the hairs on the back of my neck raised in alarm and I sensed movement. Someone was sitting on the hood of my car.

It was too dark to make out who it was, and instinctively I put my keys between my fingers the way my self-defense instructor in New Orleans had taught me.

Tell me who you are.

The person stood up. "It's Amanda."

I relaxed. Now I could see her red hair and thin frame. She looked confused as though she had just given me an answer but couldn't quite remember what the question had been. It was a look I was getting used to. I walked up to my car.

I wanted to ask her what she was doing on my car. I hadn't forgotten the way she and Stacy had treated me Monday, but then I saw that she was crying.

"Amanda, what's wrong?" I asked, genuinely concerned.

"I stayed after for NHS, but then I came out here and my car wouldn't start, and it's getting dark, and my parents are out of town, and I didn't know what I was going to do. But then you came like an answer to my prayers, except I was mean to you and you probably won't help me now." Amanda's rush of words dissolved into sobs.

I handed Amanda a tissue from my car. "Here. I'll give you a ride.'

I would give her a ride, because she needed one, and I would never forgive myself if I left her here alone. But there was no way I was the answer to any prayer. I had never been very religious, which was not surprising considering the way my mother had raised me, but I'd always believed in right and wrong, good and evil. But I'd begun to wonder which side of that equation I belonged on. My ancestors were an abomination. Maybe I was evil, and my attempts to be good were just me fighting my true nature.

Amanda looked at me in astonishment. "Really?"

"Yeah, get in," I said, and got in myself.

"Thank you, thank you, thank you."

When we were on the road I asked, "So where am I going?"

"Do you know where P Highway is?" I nodded. "I live on a little dirt road off P Highway."

I turned the car on Macarthur and headed toward Highway 72, which would take us to P just east of town. "So, why are your parents out of town?"

"Tomorrow is their anniversary, and they went down to Branson for the weekend."

"Are you going to be okay out there all by yourself? Without a car?" I flipped the rearview mirror so that the car behind me would stop blinding me. I hated having people driving behind me at night, especially trucks. They were so much higher than my little car, that they could blind you even with their low beams on, though I wasn't sure the people behind me didn't have on their brights. Some people were just considerate that way.

"Stacy is coming over tomorrow, so if I need anything she can drive me, but thanks."

"No problem," I said, scowling in the mirror at the car behind me.

Pass me.

On the next straight stretch of road, I slowed down a little, and the car behind us zoomed by. I was right. It was an SUV, and I couldn't tell, but it looked like the one from the parking lot at the school. It was some idiot I went to school with. Big surprise. I was just happy it was gone.

"Did you happen to bring home your Algebra book?" I asked.

"Yeah, why?"

"I was hoping I could borrow it. That's why I was at the school in the first place. I forgot my book, and was trying to get in and get it, but couldn't. I could bring it back before Monday, so you can get your assignment done."

Amanda dug into her backpack and pulled out a sorry looking copy of the Algebra book. "Give it to me on Monday. I did my assignment while I was sitting around hoping for a ride."

"Thank you so much."

I turned right onto P, took the dirt road Amanda said to, and was soon pulling up to Amanda's house.

"Thanks for the ride."

"Yeah, thanks for the book."

Amanda got out and I waited until she was in the house before backing out of the driveway. I was on my way back toward the pavement when I saw the SUV off in the ditch. I wasn't surprised with the way that guy had been driving. I thought about stopping, making sure they were okay, but it didn't look like it had hit anything, and it was dark and I was alone. I was considerate, but I wasn't stupid. Besides, if they needed help, they were within walking distance to several

houses. It wasn't my problem, and by the time I got back to

town I'd forgotten all about them. More evidence that I'm not

as good a person as I once thought I was.

Chapter 25

The silence that welcomed me home was a tangible thing. There were no messages on my machine, no mail in my box. Nothing.

I was done with my homework far too soon, so I did dishes, scrubbed the bathroom, and made my bed. Then there was nothing more to do.

I looked around helplessly.

Normal people aren't afraid to be alone. Normal people can just sit and do nothing sometimes. So, I sat, but within minutes I was up again pacing. I needed to keep busy. Without meaning to, I pulled my mother's necklace from its home in my pocket, and it felt as though my mother had entered the room. I stopped pacing. For a second I even thought I saw my mother's face reflected in the shiny surface of the blood red jewel, but it was just my own. I watched my own eyes reflecting back at me again and again from every red facet until my vision blurred with tears.

I was so tired. I was tired of being strong, of being responsible. I was tired of having no one to lean on, of being alone.

Then I was lying on my bed, clutching the necklace to my chest as if it was my only friend, and crying all the tears I'd been holding in since my mother's accident, since before her accident.

I cried for the time Kelly Rogers had invited everyone but me to her tenth birthday party because I didn't wear the right brand of jeans. I cried for all the times I had left a room unnoticed. I cried for all the times I'd been snubbed at Valentine parties, or moved away without a single good bye from anyone. I'd always gotten through it, believing that someday I'd find somewhere that felt like home, somewhere I belonged, and when that happened everything else would just fade into the background. That in hindsight I'd appreciate the journey for where it had led me, but in the end, it hadn't led to a place, but to a person. For me, Justin was my home and my family. I just never expected to find that my home was better off without me.

I entered the dream as if I were approaching from a great distance, floating closer and closer until I was practically right on top of a group of women. I could tell that they were sitting around discussing something, and that they had been at it for quite some time. I knew that it was some kind of meeting, but they had no bodies. It was more like they were a collection of consciouses, but it made sense in the way that everything makes sense in dreams. I stopped to hover just

313

above the group, but none of them seemed to notice my

arrival, and looking down I realized I had no body either.

The first thing I noticed was that they were all female.

The second was that each voice sounded timeless, ageless, and

beautiful as a song. They were all Sirens, and one of them

sounded familiar.

"We have to do something! We have to try at least."

"There is nothing we can do."

"Do you think she is the one?"

"I hope so."

"But we can't be sure."

"No, we can't, not until…"

"Until she joins us."

"You don't know that will happen."

"And you don't know it won't."

"I don't, but I fear that she is our last hope. His powers are growing, and if she fails the test, I fear that he will achieve his goal."

Someone whimpered. "No."

"God help us all if he does."

The dream receded from my mind as I was suddenly sucked back into consciousness. I woke up feeling more exhausted than when I'd fallen asleep. I knew I'd been dreaming, but my brain felt sluggish and the details of the dream were patchy. I got up and padded to the bathroom.

When I flipped on the light, I squinted at the sudden brightness. I hadn't checked the clock, but it was early, and my apartment was bathed in shadows, with only the slightest hint of blue showing through the blinds.

Of all of the days to get up early, I had to choose this one.

I splashed water on my face and looked in the mirror. Even with eyes that were bloodshot and puffy from crying, I somehow looked flawless, like I was going to make wet blotchy skin and unbrushed hair the new fad. Overwhelmed with my Sirenness, I closed my eyes and searched for Justin, and to my surprise I could see him.

Justin was stretched out across his bed, hugging a pillow. Lucky guy, he was still asleep. I drew closer, watching the slow rise and fall of his chest, his peaceful, relaxed face. I smiled. It was the first time I'd really smiled since the dance. Unsure if I could, I sat down on the bed beside him. All I wanted was to get closer. I missed him so much. Then, as if he sensed my presence, Justin's arm reached for me. I lay down next to him, and he put his arms around me and held me against his chest. Then the image dissolved into nothing but black and I knew it was gone.

I opened my eyes, and stared at my reflection. I wasn't sure if these visions were real or just my imagination, but I swear I could still feel the pressure of Justin's arms around me, his chin in my hair, the warmth of his chest against my cheek.

Every minute of the next two days stretched out in front of me, and with a start, I realized that Thanksgiving break was coming up in less than two weeks.

Visiting Justin's bedroom had felt so real, but it had only renewed the ache inside of me. Every time he touched me, made it that much harder to resist, that much harder to leave, and leaving Justin felt like my own heart was being ripped out of my chest. I didn't want to be alone anymore, and as I looked at my reflection I knew I wouldn't have to be. I was a Siren, and it was time I started acting like one. I wouldn't let myself have Justin, but that didn't mean I had to

be alone.

Chapter 26

The girl on the movie screen hit her attacker with the gun, but then threw it down and ran.

Why are the girls in these movies always so stupid? Doesn't she know that he's just going to pick up the gun and shoot her with it? Though based on what I'd already seen of the movie, he probably wouldn't kill her with the gun. No, that would be too easy. He'll probably just wound her enough to be able to catch her, and then take his time killing her.

Yep, there he goes. He's getting up, and there's the gun, right next to him, where she threw it. Typical.

I averted my eyes as the scene turned gory, choosing to look at our intertwined fingers instead. Casey Brown was one of the sophomores in my Spanish class, and he had unusually small hands for a boy, and they were disturbingly soft, as if he had never worked a day in his life. For all I knew he hadn't. I tried to pretend it was Justin's hand in my own, but couldn't. Justin's fingers were strong and lean and just rough enough to be manly, but not so rough that I felt inclined to rub lotion on them. I closed my eyes and tried to imagine Justin holding my hand, but the soft slick hand in mine just wasn't his, and no amount of imagination would change that. But the pressure felt surprisingly reassuring anyway.

I looked back at the movie screen. It was easier to forget who wasn't holding my hand if I focused on the movie. It was a slasher movie, and I'd chosen it because I didn't want my date feeling too amorous. It was just a date, as he'd been informed, and did not mean we had any sort of relationship beyond that. And even after explaining that too him, he'd still jumped at the chance to take me to dinner and a movie. Poor kid.

The date actually hadn't been that bad so far, especially in comparison to the horrible morning I'd had. At dinner, Casey had talked about his three older brothers who had all gone to college on baseball scholarships, and his kid sister who liked to dance. I had no family to speak of, and I'd mostly sat quietly and listened, but he didn't seem to mind. Afterward we'd driven to the Cineplex in Rolla to watch a movie, which brought me to where I was—In a dark theater holding hands with a boy I had no feelings for. But for a short time, while I'd been listening to Casey talk at dinner and in the car, I'd almost forgotten myself, and that was enough.

I had to hand it to Casey. When he'd reached for my hand when the theater lights had dimmed, it was the first physical advance he'd made all night. Even though we'd been all alone most of the night, he'd been a perfect gentleman, which some boys couldn't manage to do even in the middle of class. Someday he was going to make some girl very happy, it just wasn't going to be me.

Later, when Casey walked me to my door, I considered giving him a kiss for good behavior, but thought better of it and gave him a hug instead. The way he kept looking at my door, I knew he was hoping for more, but I said goodbye and sent him on his way. He was no Justin, but when I walked into my apartment it didn't feel quite as empty at it had before.

☐

Sunday night I went out with Ian Landers, whom I had no classes with but had run into at the gas station that morning as I was filling up my Neon. We ended up eating Subway and watching the spy drama that was at the theater in Rolla, since I had no desire to see the thriller again, and the other two were actual date movies, which I wanted to avoid.

At dinner, I took his hand when he offered and later I allowed him to put his arm around me as we watched the movie. I even went so far as to lay my head on his shoulder, and I hate to admit it, but it felt good to have an arm to support me and someone to lean on, even if it was a lie. At the end of the date, Ian leaned in for a kiss, and got a hug instead.

By Monday, I was feeling a little better. I had a friend, albeit a new one, to look forward to during the week, mindless companionship for the weekends, and the occasional imaginary rendezvous with Justin. Plus, I still had my mom, even if our conversations were strictly one sided. It wasn't what I'd have imagined for my life, but it was enough to get by. It would have to be.

When I got to school I was greeted by my usual admirers, which I politely excused myself from, so I could look for Amanda. I'd hoped to find her so I could return her book, but I couldn't find her and I didn't know where her locker was, so I headed for my locker, and hoped she would find me. I'd feel bad if I didn't get her book back to her in time, but I forgot all about Amanda's book when I saw who was waiting for me at my locker. Justin, and he didn't look happy.

"I'd ask how your weekend was, but I already know," Justin said with a sneer.

"Yeah? Because I don't think you do." I asked pushing him aside to get to my locker.

"Dates with three different guys. Believe me, I heard all the dirty little details this morning in the bathroom. What I can't understand is how it is that you can crawl into bed with anyone when you made it clear that you didn't want any relationship at all."

"Well, Mr. Know-it-all, why don't you check your facts next time before you go spouting off about things I supposedly did. I only had two dates and I didn't 'crawl' into bed with either one of them."

Justin stepped closer, invading my person space. "Are you sure, because I heard differently."

Justin's voice was low and intimate, and for an instant I remembered my brief fantasy of lying down next to him while he slept. Did he somehow know about that? Shocked I stepped back. No, of course not. One of the other boys had simply turned our goodnight hug into much more. My shock was quickly masked with anger. "Yes, I'm sure," I said with steel in my voice. "And I would have thought you, of all people, would know me better than that. Thanks for the vote of confidence. Did it ever occur to you while you were rushing out to yell at me after hearing my reputation being slandered, that you might have defended me instead?"

Justin's face fell, defeated. I'd won the argument, but I wasn't done yet.

"And just so you know, as long as you still have your mother around you will never truly know what any day of my life is really like."

I shoved my backpack into my locker and stalked off. I was still fuming when I sat down in biology.

"Winter, um…I was wondering…what are you doing tonight?"

Collin's question caught me off guard, and I couldn't help the annoyed noise that escaped my mouth. I knew I shouldn't have been surprised, but I was disappointed. Collin was my only friend at the moment, and it hurt to realize that it was over. I couldn't remain friends with him, if he was going to be asking me out every time I saw him. But, he had been a friend to me, and I hated to hurt his feelings. Luckily, Mr. Pruitt began his lecture just then, and saved me from having to answer Collin's question. I quickly turned around and threw myself into the lesson, and when class was over I raced out of class before Collin could catch up to me. I knew it wasn't a solution, but it would at least give me time to calm down before I faced him.

The rest of the morning went as usual, though the fact that I was dating seemed to have sparked hope in some who had previously not asked me out or hit on me. When lunch came around, I faced a dilemma. If I went to the library, Collin was going to finish the conversation he had started that morning, which I wasn't exactly looking forward to. But if I went to the cafeteria, I had no idea where I would sit. Carrie was still not talking to me, as far as I knew. However, to be honest, I hadn't really tried that hard to patch things up with her. Then there was Justin, whom I could tell was already in the cafeteria. I could also tell he was still angry. His anger radiated like red heat on the connection between us, and I wondered if he was still upset about our argument that morning or if something else had happened.

Curiosity got the better of me, and I followed the crowd headed for lunch. Plus, I told myself that if I saw Amanda I could give her back her book.

The moment I walked through the lunchroom doors, I knew something was up. I instantly spotted Justin in his usual spot with the other athletes. He was listening to something Billy Thompson was saying, with a clenched jaw and narrow eyes. His anger was obvious even to others around him. Carrie was sitting next to him looking just as upset. Then Justin's eyes met mine, and I knew without a doubt, what Billy was talking about—me.

Surprisingly I wasn't too mad about it. It wasn't the first time Billy had said horrible things about me. I gave Justin a tight-lipped smile to tell him I understood before looking for Amanda at the other end of the room. When I didn't see her, I left without getting a tray. I'd had enough of the cafeteria already.

Chapter 27

On the way to the parking lot after school, Brittany caught up with me.

"Hey," she said.

"Aren't you violating some sisterhood friendship law or something by talking to me?"

"You mean because of Carrie? Naa, she'll get over it. Besides, she's not really mad at you anyway."

"You could have fooled me," I said and kept trudging along to my car on the far end of the lot.

"You and I are double dating this Friday."

I gave her a wary look. "Aren't you afraid I'm going to steal your date?"

"If you do then I'll just take yours. It's not like it really matters, but I'm not too worried about it. You aren't the only

Siren around here." Brittany whispered the word Siren, so I would be the only one to hear.

I met her dark green eyes, and saw a bit of a challenge in them. "Sure," I said, "you're on. This Friday night. So, what are we doing?"

"I want to go dancing. Have you ever been to Millennium?"

"That club in Rolla? No, don't you have to be twenty-one to get in?"

"Yeah. So?"

"Well, the last time I checked, my driver's license says in big purple letters that I'm under twenty-one. I think they'll notice."

"Just leave it to me. And if my charms don't work, you can always work your magic." Brittany shrugged like it was no big deal.

I rolled my eyes. "Whatever."

Brittany started to leave and I called out to her, "Thanks for inviting me."

"Don't worry about it. We're sisters," Brittany called back to me. "And, Winter? You should really talk to Carrie."

☐

I was doing the dishes, with the TV on for company, when I heard the news.

"Police dogs and search teams are combing the Mark Twain National Forest, near where the teenager was last seen," A female reporter said, and I turned to watch as people with flashlights fanned out behind her. "Amanda Perdue, of Salem, has been missing now for at least two days if not more. She was last seen heading for her car in the Salem High School parking lot around 4:30 p.m. on Friday of last week. If anyone has any information about her whereabouts, they can call our tip line…"

The report continued, but I didn't hear any more. The plate I had been washing dropped from my hand and broke on the floor, and a sob escaped my lips.

Amanda was missing, and I was the last one to see her.

Suddenly, the things I'd been so worried about seemed trivial, so selfish. I was about to call the tip line to tell them everything I knew when the phone rang. The caller ID said it was Amanda.

"Thank goodness! I just saw that you were missing on the news. Are you all right? Where are you?"

When I paused to take a breath, I realized that Amanda hadn't said anything. In fact, the other end of the line was quiet except for some strange noises that sounded like the scrape of dead leaves over pavement. The hair on my arms stood up.

"Amanda?"

Someone male on the other line laughed, and my skin crawled. Then there was a click, and a dial tone.

Someone else had Amanda's cell phone. Someone male, and she was missing. I felt like I was going to be sick. I nearly jumped out of my skin when the phone rang again.

"Hello?" I answered without checking who it was.

"Winter?"

"Collin," I said relieved.

"Are you okay? You sounded worried."

"I'm fine," I said, thinking of how much worse I could be. "But, I really can't talk right now. I have to make a phone call. It's important."

"Okay, but will you please call me when you can?"

"Sure. I've got to go."

I hung up the phone and took a deep breath. Then I dialed 911. Within minutes, the police were at my apartment to get my statement.

"So, you claim that you just got a phone call from Amanda Perdue's cell phone?" asked the grim-faced officer. His badge said Officer Webster.

"Yes, but she didn't say anything, and then a man laughed, at least I think it was a man. I don't know, it happened so fast," I said feeling flustered.

Officer Webster went to check my phone, while the other one, the one with a mustache, looked around the room. "You live here alone?"

"Yes, I'm emancipated. My mother is in a coma."

Officer Webster raised an eyebrow, and looked at me. "Your caller ID says Collin Greene. Was he the one you heard laugh?"

"No, he called me right after the other call. Before I could call you guys." This wasn't going well.

Mustached officer, who has been taking notes, held up an Algebra book. "If you live alone, why are there two books?"

"It's Amanda's book…"

"The missing girl's book?"

"Yes, she let me borrow it Friday night when I gave her a ride home…"

"Friday night? What time was this?"

"I don't know, around six maybe? But the phone call, she's in trouble…"

"How well do you know Amanda Perdue?" Officer Webster asked.

"We were kind of friends, up until a few weeks ago…"

"What happened? Did you have a fight?"

"No, I just found other friends…"

"If you aren't friends anymore, how is it that you were giving her a ride home?"

"Pure luck. I forgot my book, and her car had broken down, and she needed a ride…"

"Was the book payment for getting a ride?"

"No, what?"

"Where did you take Amanda Friday night?"

"I took her home."

"Were there any witnesses, anyone see you pick her up or drop her off?"

"No, the school was deserted. But wait, yes, there was one car. A dark colored SUV. A Bronco I think. It was there in the parking lot of the school, and they saw me drop her off at home too."

"How is that? Do you know the person driving? Was it a boyfriend or one of your new friends?"

"No. I don't know who it was, but they were a terrible driver. They rode my bumper half the way there, before they finally passed me. But then I saw them off in a ditch near her neighbor's house. I think they live in one of the houses on Amanda's road. Why else would they have been out that far?"

"Off in a ditch? Do you suffer from road rage, Miss Loveless?"

"No, I didn't run them off the road or anything…"

Officer Mustache closed his notebook. "I think we have heard enough. Miss, do you realize that if you did indeed

338

give Amanda a ride home on Friday night that you were possibly the last person to see her before she disappeared?"

"Yes," I said with a hollow voice.

"We'll keep in touch," Officer Webster said, and they left.

I felt exhausted, as if I'd just endured a great beating. As I sat there with my head in my hands, going over everything that had just happened two things occurred to me. 1. They thought I was lying about the phone call. 2. The cops thought I'd done something to Amanda.

Chapter 28

The next day, everyone at school was talking about it, and I mean everyone. Jocks, cheerleaders, smart kids, goofballs, the artsy kids, everyone. People who had never noticed Amanda when she was there, were suddenly super aware of her absence, and I watched it all silently. It almost felt like old times, except that I was far from invisible. Word had spread that I was the last person to see Amanda. And all of those girls who hated me because their boyfriends noticed me when I entered a room or would turn their heads to watch me walk down the hall, now had ammunition they needed to attack me.

When I got to school on Tuesday, I noticed that groups of girls would begin whispering when I walked by or would stop talking altogether. I ignored them. I had more important things on my mind than petty little girls and their gossip.

The news that morning had said that Amanda's parents had returned home Sunday evening, and Amanda was gone. Nothing was missing but the clothes she was wearing and her car, which had later been found in the school parking lot. There was no sign of a struggle and the house had been locked. So, the general belief was that Amanda had left willingly, with someone she knew. I wasn't so sure.

I couldn't get that SUV out of my mind. They had been there when I picked Amanda up, and they had followed us to her house. I had a sinking feeling that whoever had been driving that car knew what had happened to Amanda.

☐

At lunchtime, I put aside my fear that Collin would ask me out, and went to the library. I needed a friend, and I realized that I'd never called him back, and I wanted to explain.

I found Collin sitting reading a book, and I plopped down beside him.

"Hey, how are you doing?" Collin asked, putting his book away.

He really was a nice guy. I was there to apologize and he was still worried about how I was doing.

"I'm okay, I guess. I'm sorry I didn't call you back yesterday. I'd just heard about Amanda, and…"

"Don't worry about it. It wasn't that important. I can talk to you about it some other time," Collin said.

"Are you sure?"

"Yeah."

I'd been willing to hear what he had to say, but secretly, or maybe not so secretly, I was relieved to not have to. I really did like Collin, and I didn't want to hurt him, but I just didn't feel that way about him.

"So, where are Marc and Thomas?"

"They prefer the chemistry room."

"Really?" I asked, skeptical.

"Well, I may have had something to do with it," Collin admitted.

"So, why aren't you with them?"

"I was hoping to spend my lunch with you," Collin said a little shyly.

I blushed. It was sweet but it made me feel bad for avoiding him the day before.

The rest of the lunch period was quieter than usual. Each of us seemed lost in our own thoughts, but the silences

343

were comfortable ones, and I was happy just to have someone to sit with.

☐

After school, I went to see my mom, and was surprised to see that someone had replaced her irises with a bouquet of blue carnations. Justin.

I smiled and squeezed my mom's hand. I was glad that she was getting visitors. I know it's crazy, since she was in a coma, but I didn't want to tell my mom what was going on, because I didn't want her to worry about me. So instead, I told her about how the trees were changing colors, and how warm it had been that day compared to the previous week. Then I sat and watched the sky outside my mom's window go from blue to orange to a light shade of magenta before I left for home.

The message light was flashing when I walked in the door, and after setting down my jacket and backpack I went over to the little phone table to listen to it.

I pushed play and waited for the message to begin, and the longer I waited the more nervous I got. Then, just before the answering machine cut off the call, a muffled voice spoke.

"I know what you are…" The voice whispered and my blood ran cold. I was frozen with fear, and by the time it occurred to me that I should save the message, the machine had already erased it.

The man who had Amanda's phone had called again. I found myself wondering if he had harassed Amanda before he had taken her, because at this point I was sure he had taken her.

What does he mean, 'he knows what I am'? Or did he say who I am?

I didn't know, but I did know I didn't want to be alone anymore. So I called up Nick from my Algebra class and told him that on second thought I'd love to go out with him.

Chapter 29

The twenty minutes it took Nick to pick me up took forever. I kept going from sitting to pacing to sitting again. I checked the parking lot in front of my building every couple of minutes. Whether I was looking for Nick or for the dark SUV I wasn't sure, and for a moment I was frozen with the fear that Nick would be driving the dark SUV. Because for all I knew it could be anyone. But then Nick pulled up in a red pickup truck, and I breathed a sigh of relief.

We went to the movie theater in Rolla, because that seems to be what you do on a date. But once we got there, I realized that I'd already seen two of the movies and didn't want to see the other two. So, I crossed my fingers, a habit I'd picked up from my mom, and let Nick pick while I went to the concession stand to get popcorn. When Nick came back with tickets to the slasher movie, I wasn't sure if the crossed fingers had worked or not, but at least it wasn't a romance.

We'd just settled into our seats when I noticed someone sitting low in their seat in the back of the theater with a baseball cap pulled down over their eyes. I was already on edge, wondering who had taken Amanda, and whether I was next on their list. So, my fear sensors pricked up at the odd behavior. But then there was something familiar about the shape of the shoulders, and the way the boy was sitting that caught me off guard. Afraid I'd get caught staring, I turned around to face the screen, but couldn't put the boy out of my mind. I felt drawn to him. A minute later I snuck a peek at the boy and nearly choked on my soft drink. It was Justin. I'd been so preoccupied with other things that I hadn't realized how close he felt.

The moment I realized who it was I scrunched down in my own seat, hoping he hadn't seen me. The idea of me dating other boys hadn't gone over so well, so I didn't want to run into him while I was actually on a date. I took Nick's hand and tried to act normal, but I was self-conscious of everything I did, and couldn't help wondering if Justin had followed me.

No, that's crazy. It's just a popular movie, and he's hiding in the back because he doesn't want anyone recognizing him and knowing he went to the movies by himself. I'd feel uncomfortable going to the movies by my self.

When the movie was over, I took my time gathering my purse and coat, and when we finally left, Justin was gone. Either he hadn't seen me, or he hadn't wanted to stop to chat. Whatever the reason, I was saved from a confrontation I'd rather avoid.

When Nick had gotten the, now usual, goodnight hug, and I was again home alone, every shadow seemed to jump out at me. The horror movie had been a bad idea. I was even more jumpy than I had been before. So, I did what I used to do when I was little. I got into bed and pretended that the bad things hiding in the shadows couldn't see me if I didn't move, and the next thing I knew it was morning.

☐

Wednesday went much the same as Tuesday, except that the girls at school were even more hostile than they had been the day before, going so far as to bump into me on 'accident' in the halls, and to block my way as I entered or exited class. They actually made me late to a couple of my classes, but I kept it to myself. I knew they were hoping I'd complain to a teacher, and I wasn't going to give them that satisfaction. Plus, I knew that if it got really bad I could change their behavior really fast. At lunch Collin and I kept to safe subjects, and though I half expected Justin to come storming up to me again, he didn't. In fact, I didn't see him at all, that is, until that night.

I didn't want to be alone, and I didn't even want to go home, so I talked Brandon, a boy from my English class, into taking me out right after school. I went home only long enough to drop off my car, before we headed for Rolla.

I was tired of the theater, so we went bowling instead. They must have been having some sort of promotional night, because the place was packed with college kids, but they found us a lane in the middle next to a boy with dark hair and gray eyes who looked vaguely familiar. I went to get a ball from the rack near his lane as I tried to figure out where I'd seen him before. Then it hit me, he worked at the theater. He noticed me looking at him, and I gave him an awkward smile, and quickly went back to my lane.

I'd just bowled my first frame, when I saw Justin lacing up a pair of bowling shoes four lanes over. Again, he didn't acknowledge me, and he was alone. I ignored him and tried to focus on Brandon. I got mostly gutter balls, but Brandon was actually pretty good at bowling. And as much as I tried to pretend I wasn't paying attention, I noticed that Justin wasn't bad either. I don't know if Brandon noticed, but every time he got a strike, Justin seemed a little more intent on getting one himself. In the end, I got a score of 67, and Brandon got a 135. I didn't get to see Justin's score, but I would have sworn he was smiling when he left.

Chapter 30

I was feeling a little better when Brandon left me at my door. Note to self: When you are scared, bowling works better than a scary movie to lighten your mood. I was actually smiling when I unlocked the door, but my mood deflated like a popped balloon when I saw the blinking red light on my answering machine.

It's probably nothing. Maybe it's Justin calling to say he saw me at the bowling alley.

But I didn't check my messages. I left the light blinking at me from across the room, like some kind of warning. I knew I'd have to listen to it eventually, but I wanted to feel safe for a little while longer, before I faced reality. So, I made myself a snack and took a shower. When I was dressed in my flannel pajamas, I knew it was time. So, clutching my mom's necklace, I slowly made my way over to the machine and pushed the button.

Then an automated voice said, "This message is for Teniqua Jeffers. If you are Teniqua Jeffers please press one now. If you are not Teniqua Jeffers please press two…"

It was the wrong number. I felt a weight rise off me, and soon I was laughing. It was just a wrong number. I was wiping tears out of my eyes, when a second beep made me realize there was another call. I stopped.

There was no laugh, no voice, no anything, but something about the silence sent a shiver down my spine. It wasn't a hang up call. Who ever had called, had waited, listening until the machine had cut them off. The caller ID revealed nothing.

I hastily hit delete. I'd decided that if I got any more calls I'd save them for the police to hear, but somehow, I knew that they wouldn't think the silent caller was as sinister as I did. It would probably just make them think I was crazier then they already thought I was.

I was walking away when the answering machine beeped again, and a third message began to play.

"Winter, I know you are kind of avoiding me, but we need to talk. It's about a guy, and I'm worried about you, and I know this doesn't make any sense, but I know something is going on. I know…things. Please, just call me."

Justin's message ended and I deleted it. I had enough to deal with, without worrying about his jealousy right now. I'd talk to him later when things had gotten less crazy. Then I thought about what he'd said.

Why was everyone suddenly telling me they knew things? It was such a cryptic thing to say, and it made me nervous.

I closed my eyes and tried to see Justin, but nothing happened. Though I could still feel him somewhere across town, probably safe in his own bed, all I could see was darkness.

□

Early the next morning the weather turned cold, and the entire area was under a winter weather advisory. Everyone at school was talking about the four or five inches of accumulation we were supposed to get, and it made me want to laugh. Yeah, it was cold but it had been close to seventy degrees two days ago. Even if we did get snow, there was no way it would stick, but I didn't bother correcting anyone. As long as they were talking about the weather, they couldn't talk about me. But then someone brought up the fact that Amanda was still missing, and quite possibly out in the woods somewhere and suddenly the weather report wasn't so laughable.

Since I'd never felt the need to have a cell phone, at lunchtime I had to use the payphone in the front lobby to call the police. I needed to know if they had any new leads, but whether they did or not they weren't about to share that information with me. When I finally made it to the library, I suggested to Collin that we should go looking for her.

"Winter, I know it's terrible to imagine her out there in this weather, but the cops are searching. We have to let them do their job. If we went hiking through the woods right now it would only make things harder on them, because then they'd have to search for three people instead of one."

I wasn't happy about it, but I knew he was right. I knew nothing about hiking and the Mark Twain National Forest covered most of the state. Getting lost in the woods was no small deal, but I still felt antsy. I wanted to be doing something.

At the end of the day, I found Justin waiting for me by my locker. I tried to act indifferent, but my pounding heart betrayed me. I just hoped it wasn't as loud to him as it was to me.

I could tell it had started snowing because I could see a few flakes lingering in his dark hair, and his t-shirt was peppered with little wet spots where it stretched tight across his shoulders. His eyes were boring a hole right through me, but I wouldn't meet his gaze. Instead, I found myself staring at his mouth, remembering the feel of it on my own. The urge to kiss him again was almost unbearable. With burning cheeks, I shifted my gaze to my shoes.

"Are you going out again tonight?" Justin asked, his mouth set in a thin line.

"I don't know."

"Don't go out tonight."

I had been considering actually staying home that night, but there is just something about being told what to do that makes me want to do the opposite. "Too bad, I already made plans," I said defiantly.

"Winter, you can't go out tonight," Justin said stepping closer, backing me up against my locker.

Now I was determined to go out. "Too bad, it's not up to you."

"Winter, you can't…I can't…" Justin turned away and dragged his hands through his hair. "I have practice tonight, and I can't miss it."

Now I understood. I couldn't go out, because he had a game. And if he was at a game, then he couldn't follow me.

"Good for you. I'm going dancing," I said drawing on tomorrow's plans with Brittany because I honestly hadn't made any for that night. Then my mouth took it one step further. "with Collin Greene."

Why I chose him, I wasn't sure, but it was out there and I couldn't take it back. I just hoped I could get him to skip Quiz Bowl practice, and actually go with me.

"Winter, please just trust me," Justin said taking my hands in his, sending an electric current blazing up both arms.

The logical part of my brain was screaming at me to run away as fast as possible, but I didn't want to. All I wanted was to hold on to him a little longer, to feel his hands on mine. I found myself staring up into his dark eyes, unable to say or do anything.

"Please, Winter," Justin pleaded, "please, for me."

"Justin, I…" I said, finding my voice, "I'll think about it."

Justin looked like he might press me further, but then thought better of it. Then he released my hands to search the pockets of his jacket, and slipped something into my hand. "I was going to leave this in your locker for you, but here." Justin took two steps and turned back to look at me with sad eyes that made my heart break into a million pieces. "I know you don't want to hear it, but…"

Justin, please don't. Please don't say it. I sent the thought but my heart wasn't really in it, and I knew it was weak.

"…I love you."

I wanted to tell him how much I loved him, how much I needed him, but he was already gone, having left me standing there like a quivering bowl of melted butter. Then I

361

felt something in my hand, and I remembered his gift. I was

holding a Baby Ruth candy bar. It was a peace offering.

Chapter 31

I had never been to a club before, but Millennium looked about what I expected a club to look like: dark, smoky, and dirty around the edges. Strobe lights flashed in time as the techno version of some song (that sounded vaguely familiar) blasted from the speakers. I could feel the bass vibrating the floor beneath my feet. It wasn't the type of place I would have thought I'd like, but the combination of lights and music was intoxicating, and I found myself wanting to forget the cold outside, and Amanda, and the creepy phone calls, and just let loose on the dance floor.

I hadn't planned on actually going out. After speaking with Justin, and seeing how upset he was, I really had intended to stay home. But something about the snow softly falling outside and the utter silence of my apartment made me think of *The Shining*, and when the phone rang, I almost jumped out of my skin.

It was Collin, calling to tell me that quiz bowl practice had gotten out early because of the weather, and then before I'd really thought it through I'd invited him to go out with me. Then I'd had to call Brittany and see if she wanted to change our plans, and to my relief she was all for it.

So, that was how I found myself on the dance floor with an awkward and uncomfortable looking Collin, who was standing about two feet away from me stepping from one foot to the other in that way that guys who can't dance dance. As soon as the song ended, though I say ended loosely, because it was more like it merged into a different song, Collin jumped at the opportunity to nab one of the few tables tucked into the corners around the dance floor.

I sat down feeling flushed. I hadn't moved that much in a long time. I could stay on rhythm with the music, but I was not what most would call a good dancer. But that didn't seem to matter anymore, everyone around us kept looking at me like I was some pop star's backup dancer.

I was surprised when Brittany and her date, Darren, sat down next to us, because they could have been some pop star's backup dancers. But I guess even the professionals need a break now and then.

"Oh my, is it hot in here?" Brittany said, fanning herself.

"It's just you, Babe," Darren said, though I could see the perspiration on his forehead sparkling in the neon lights.

"Darren, Sweetie, why don't you go get me a coke," Brittany said, and like that Darren was out of his chair, headed toward the bar.

"That was fast," I said, leaning close so she could hear me over the music.

"Yeah, I might just have to keep this one around," she yelled back to me.

"Do you want anything to drink?" Collin asked, leaning close to my ear. I wasn't sure if he asked because he saw Darren getting Brittany a drink and thought he should follow suit, or if it was just because a new song had started and he was trying to avoid dancing.

It turns out Collin didn't like dancing. He was okay with the walk in a circle type of slow dancing, but club dancing not so much. I'd had to beg him to come with me, and he'd only agreed after I'd assured him that I couldn't dance either. But after the first song it was obvious he thought I'd been lying about not being a good dancer. Now I was sure I'd have to use all of my charm if I wanted to get him back on the dance floor.

"Yeah, a water would be great," I said.

When he'd gone, Brittany turned to me and said something.

"What?" I yelled back to her.

"I said, isn't this great?"

I smiled in response. I was having fun, but as soon as one of the tables by the door opened up, I was taking it. We were so close to the speakers that I could feel the little hairs at the base of my head being blown back by the music, and I could already envision the hearing aids I would need when I was older.

Brittany took a few drinks, and then she and Darren were back on the dance floor gyrating in time with the slow steady pulse of the next song. I looked toward the bar, but couldn't find Collin anywhere. I checked the lines at the bathrooms, and the dance floor, but still no Collin. Apprehension was setting in when he finally flopped down in the chair beside me.

"I was beginning to think you'd ditched me," I said, turning to Collin, but finding Justin sitting beside me.

"I would never do something like that," Justin said watching me intently. His gaze traveled the length of my body, and I was suddenly ultra aware of every inch of skin left exposed by the dress I'd borrowed from Brittany. "Would you like to dance?"

I glanced around one last time for Collin, but he was nowhere to be seen. "Sure."

Justin took my hand and led me to a corner of the room opposite the speakers, where the music wasn't quite so deafening.

"What are you doing here?" Justin asked.

"Dancing, what does it look like?"

"How'd you even get in? They card at the door?"

"Brittany can be very persuasive when she wants to be."

"Yeah, I'm sure she can."

"What's that supposed to mean?"

Justin looked me in the eye. "Exactly what it sounds like."

I looked away, uncomfortable. "You're here too, so what's your story?"

"I slipped the guy a twenty."

"Oh," I said, feeling stupid. I would have to remember that for next time. "Anyway, I thought you said you had practice," I added, trying desperately to act indifferent to the closeness of his body and his hands on my waist.

369

"I did," Justin said, pulling me closer, as if daring me to keep acting unaffected by his proximity now that we were chest to chest. Inside my emotions were reeling, but with great effort, I kept on the mask of indifference.

"Then how is it that you are here dancing with me?"

"I quit the team," Justin said, dipping me with a skill I never knew he possessed, before bringing me back up to face him.

"What?" I said, too surprised to keep up the facade. "But what about trying to get a scholarship? How are you going to pay for college?"

I knew that Justin's mom could afford to buy him name brand clothes and a decent car on her income, but when it came to higher education, they were crossing their fingers hoping for a scholarship.

"There is always next year. Besides, this wouldn't have happened if you had just listened to me."

"Don't even blame this on me. I didn't make you come here."

"No, I chose that because some things are more important than basketball, or even what college I go to."

"And what things would those be?"

We had stopped dancing by now, but Justin had me backed against the wall.

"Do I really have to spell it out for you? You, Winter. Your safety."

My sense of apprehension returned. "What do you mean my safety?"

"Winter, someone is following you."

"I know," I said, looking him up and down, "He's about six foot one, with dark hair, and dark eyes."

"Not me, someone else," Justin said, his voice getting quiet.

"Justin, I know you've been following me. Don't even try to deny it, because I've seen you."

"I'm not denying it. I'm saying someone else is following you, and…," he stopped and looked away.

"And what?" I asked incredulously.

Justin met my eyes and I saw the muscle in his jaw flex. "And he wants to hurt you."

"What do you mean?"

"There is a man following you around, and he wants to…hurt you."

"Justin, you're scaring me. What are you talking about?"

"Winter, just trust me. I know what I'm talking about."

"How do you know?"

Justin drew me to him, caressing my face in his hands, and with tears in his eyes he said, "Because, I've heard it. I've *seen* it. I've seen you die over and over again in my head."

I stiffened in his arms. The phone calls. The dark SUV. Someone *was* following me. Deep down I knew it was true. Those calls were no joke or prank, but how did Justin know anything about it? The only one I'd seen following me was him. But then he had been acting strange lately, and he drove a blue Blazer…No! I couldn't believe Justin wanted to hurt me. It had to be a lucky guess. It was just a ploy to get me back. A creepy ploy, but a ploy just the same.

"I know you don't believe me, but I've heard and seen it in his mind. I can hear his thoughts," Justin said looking exhausted, "just like I can hear yours now."

An icy chill crept down my spine. "What?"

"Winter, I…"

Did he just tell me he could read minds? Two months ago, I would have laughed at the possibility, but now…

Justin laughed but there was no humor in it. "I know what you're thinking, and no I can't read all minds—just his…and *yours*," Justin said and held my gaze.

"This is crazy. You didn't just read my mind. That was a coincidence. Anyone would have been thinking the same thing."

"Would they? Then test me."

"Fine. I bet you can't tell me what I'm thinking right now." I wiped all emotion but defiance from my face, and let my mind think the three words I'd been suppressing for so long.

I love you.

Justin took my face in his hands again, and brushed his thumb across my lips. "I know, but I wish I could hear it from your lips as well."

My knees where trembling. *It was true. But if he could hear my thoughts, how much did he know? How much had he heard?* My chest felt tight. There wasn't enough air.

"Winter, calm down."

Why can't I breathe?

"You're hyperventilating. Just calm down, and breathe."

Did he just answer my thoughts? Okay, breathe. Breathe.

"Winter?"

The sound of my name startled me out of my panic attack, and looking over Justin's shoulder I found Collin.

"Collin!" I broke away from Justin and went to Collin's side. "I looked all over for you. Where've you been?"

Collin held out a bottle of water. "I got you a drink."

"Thanks." I took the bottle.

"Justin." Collin said, acknowledging Justin, though he didn't look happy about it.

Justin eyed Collin just as warily. "Collin."

"Come on, Collin, let's dance," I said.

I needed some space from Justin. I needed to be able to think, and to my surprise, Collin took my arm without argument. I had a feeling that Justin's presence had something to do with his willingness to dance, but at the moment I thought it best not to point that out. As we walked away, I chanced a look over my shoulder at Justin. He hadn't moved and he was watching me with an intensity that was a little frightening. I still wasn't sure what to make of what he'd told me, but I decided to test him further.

Justin, don't look at me like you are going to carry me away caveman style. I'm surrounded by people. What's the worst that could happen? Besides, I'm with Collin. I trust Collin. I just need some time to think. It's a lot to take in.

Justin nodded, and sat down, though he didn't take his eyes off me.

I felt short of breath again.

He'd heard me. He really could hear my thoughts.

I felt the panic rising within me again, and Justin gave me a look that said, "Really? Are you doing this again?"

I decided it was best to look away. If he answered my thoughts again I was going to pass out.

"Collin, I'm sorry about Justin," I said, trying to sound as though each breath wasn't taking all of my concentration.

"If it's alright, I'd rather not talk about him," Collin said and for the first time I noticed how close we were dancing. Collin was practically on top of me, and he was holding me much more intimately than he had less than an hour ago. Was he trying to make Justin jealous, or had he somehow misunderstood when I'd told him we were just friends?

"Okay, what would you like to talk about?" I asked uncertain.

"This."

Collin's mouth on mine cut off any response I might have had. For a moment, I was too shocked to even think, but then the only thought going through my head was, *No, this can't be happening. I have to stop this.*

It wasn't that he was a bad kisser, he was just different from Justin, and part of me wanted to enjoy it, to give him a chance, but it just felt wrong. I didn't feel that way for Collin.

But when I tried to pull back, he kissed me with more urgency.

"Stop…Collin…stop!" I managed to get out, but his hands on my shoulders held me in place and I couldn't get away.

Stop!

The next thing I knew, Justin was beside me, and Collin was on the floor with blood streaming from his nose.

"Collin! Are you alright?"

A crowd had formed around us. I took the napkins someone handed to me, and held them to Collin's nose. Then I looked up at Justin. "Why'd you do that? You didn't have to hit him!"

"That's the thanks I get? Fine, I'm out of here!" Justin stalked off ignoring the bouncer who had come to break up the fight.

"Justin, wait," I called after him, but he was gone and the crowd was pressing even closer. It was just as well, because I had no idea what I would say to him. So he could read my mind, but that didn't change the fact that he didn't really love me.

I helped Collin to his feet, and he blinked at me as if even he didn't know what had just happened.

"Don't worry, we're going," I said as the bouncer approached.

Chapter 32

I had never been to Collin's house before. Earlier I'd picked him up from the school, but by the time we got back from Rolla he still had dried blood around his nose and one of his eyes was beginning to swell shut. And though he hadn't technically invited me in, I wasn't going to leave him alone like that. So, when he unlocked his front door, I followed him inside. I found the kitchen and began searching his freezer for ice for his face, but the tray was empty so I grabbed a bag of frozen corn instead.

"Here," I said, handing him the corn.

He looked at it confused.

"It's for your face."

He put the corn over his eye and then neither of us knew what to say. As I stood there awkwardly, I took in

Collin's house. It was a nice house, not fancy, but nice. The kitchen was clean and full of little personal items that made it feel homey. One particular picture on the refrigerator caught my eye. It was a picture of Collin and someone who could only be his mom, but she looked very familiar. Where had I seen her before?

"Winter, I'm sorry about what happened...at Millennium."

"Look, it's okay. I understand."

"No, it wasn't what you think. It was like I had no control of my own body."

"I know it's hard, sometimes, for guys to control themselves around me lately. Don't worry about it."

"That's the thing...Winter, there's something I've been wanting to talk to you about," Collin said, getting my attention, but I found my eyes straying back to the picture. I was sure I knew her from somewhere.

"Collin, is this your mom?"

"That's kind of what I wanted to talk to you about."

"Your mom?" That wasn't what I would have thought he wanted to talk about.

"My mom is a Siren."

He had my attention now. "What did you say?"

"I know…well, I think I know what has been going on between you and Justin, and I just want you to know that you don't have to worry about that with me, because my mom is like you, and I know you aren't interested in me like that, but I want you to know that I think you're beautiful and amazing for who you are and not what you are, and…"

"Collin, one thing at a time. First of all, you knew about me? And you never told me?"

"Not at first, but the way everyone at school has been acting, it wasn't too hard to guess. Then I asked my mom just to make sure."

"Your mom," I looked at the picture again, and then I remembered. "Beth, from the funeral."

"She's been hoping she could see you again, but you can understand why I haven't invited you over yet."

"Okay, so your mom is a Siren," I said, trying not to have another panic attack. "But what does that have to do with me and Justin?"

"I'm a son of a Siren."

"So."

"You really don't know, do you?"

"It's not like there's a class to take on this sort of stuff," I said annoyed.

"Sons of Sirens are immune to the call. It's like an inborn safety feature to protect us from falling in love with our sister or our mom. Winter, you don't have to worry about it being real with me."

A line from my mother's diary flitted through my mind. *I felt it leave me.*

"Are you saying that all boys born with the power are immune to me?"

"Yeah."

"Wait, do you have any powers yourself?"

"No, I'm just a carrier. My first daughter will get it all."

"Are you sure? You don't have any special abilities?"

"No, I mean sometimes a son of a Siren will get some heightened senses but not usually."

"Collin, I've got to go," I said, and rushed for the door.

"Wait, I've got something for you."

I waited for what felt like an eternity, though it was probably only a few seconds. When Collin came back, he dropped my mother's necklace into my hand.

"Where did you…?"

"You always take it out and hold it when you're upset. You left it in the library after lunch today," Collin said with a shy smile, and I noticed he had dimples.

"Thank you."

"It's just, I know it means a lot to you, and I didn't want you getting upset when you realized it was gone."

"It was my mom's…Thank you. I have to go."

"Good luck with him," Collin said, and I leaned in and gave Collin a kiss on the cheek. I knew it wasn't what he was hoping for, but it would have to do.

When I got back into my car, I drove off in a hurry, and was speeding down the road before I realized that I didn't even know for sure where I was going. I had to find Justin. I had to know if he was immune too. I decide to start with his house.

I probably broke every traffic law as I raced over to Justin's house. If Justin was immune, then every touch, every kiss…Oh, I needed to see Justin now, if he'd still see me.

Chapter 33

"Mrs. Smith, could I talk to Justin please?"

My heart was pounding, my hands shaking.

Mrs. Smith gave me a confused look. "Justin isn't here. His practices sometimes run long."

She didn't know he'd quit yet.

"Oh."

"Do you want to wait here for him to come home? Or would you like me to give him a message?"

"No, I just wanted to see him, thanks. I guess I'll see him tomorrow," I said trying to hide the twinge of panic I was feeling. He should have been home by now, but that didn't necessarily mean anything. There was no need to make his mom worry.

I drove to the stop sign at the end of the road, before the panic overwhelmed me, and I couldn't see due to the tears streaming down my face.

Justin had said someone was following me. If I noticed Justin following me, then my stalker probably had too. Why hadn't I listened?

I've got to find him. Where would he be? He could be anywhere.

I closed my eyes and tried to see him, but all I saw was the back of my own eyelids. I could still feel him, but just barely. He was far away.

Think. Think. Think. How did I see him before? There has to be a connection. The first two times were at night, but the last time was in the morning. The first and second time I was in the shower, but not the third. The third time I'd just woke up, and was at the sink washing my face…Water. Water had to be the connection.

A car behind me honked, forcing me to keep driving, but as soon as I got through the intersection, I pulled off the road.

I needed some water, but my car's cup holders were empty, and I remembered that I'd cleaned out my car after school. Then I remembered the bottle of water Collin had gotten for me, but I must have left it at the club because when I looked in my purse it wasn't there. Frustrated, I slammed my fist into my steering wheel.

Amanda's missing, Justin's gone, and Collin thinks he's in love with me, and on top of all of that, it was sleeting. I could hear the little pieces pelting my car as the slushy snow that had been falling all day turned into ice.

Snow. Ice. Water.

I looked out at the dusting of snow on the grass and the ice that had begun to accumulate at the edges of my windshield. I was surrounded by water.

I got out of my car and held my hands out. Within seconds my fingers were wet and red with cold, but I ignored it. I closed my eyes.

I was outside in the woods somewhere, and lying in the mud at my feet was Justin. His eyes were closed and there was blood on his face, though I couldn't tell where it had come from. At first, I was afraid he was dead, but I could tell from the little puffs of steam coming from his nose that he was breathing.

That's when I realized that I had feet. I'd never seen myself in one of these visions before, and I'd kind of assumed I was just a floating conscious, like in my dreams, if these visions were real at all. But looking down I could see my chunky high heels, and my skinny legs, but they were transparent, or rather translucent. I looked like a pencil outline of myself. I was all grays and whites, dark around the edges and kind of see through in the center.

☐

I knelt beside Justin, reached out to touch his face, and was surprised when my hand didn't go straight through him. I could feel him, and I wondered if he could see me, feel me. Then I remembered that the first couple of times I'd seen Justin this way, I'd been in the shower, and I rather hoped that he couldn't.

I looked around. The branches above me were devoid of leaves, however they still provided some shelter from the sleet and snow coming down so that the ground was wet, but it wasn't yet covered in the snow that had begun to accumulate everywhere else. To my right I could see a break in the trees. I hated to leave Justin, but I needed to find out where he was. So with one last look at Justin's peaceful face, I got up and headed for the clearing.

When I broke through the line of trees, I was surprised to find that I wasn't in a clearing at all, but on the banks of a stream. The snow had drifted on the far bank and along the edge of the forest, but the stream still flowed freely. Across the river and a little ways up stream, I could just make out an outcropping of rocks through the trees.

I opened my eyes and jumped back into my car, cranking up the heat. I knew exactly where Justin was. I just hoped I could find it again.

On the north end of town, I came to an intersection where the road split like a river around an island in its path. I didn't remember if I was supposed to go right or left. I pulled into the little service station between the roads, but it was locked up. Where was a Seven Eleven when I needed one?

I rushed to the payphone by the door and dialed 911.

"911. What's your emergency?"

"My friend has been kidnapped and needs help."

"I'm sorry, what's your name," the operator went on in the same dull voice.

"Winter, but that doesn't matter. You need to send someone to the river. Dent's Ford, I think."

"Calm down, Winter. Tell me what's happened."

"My best friend has been kidnapped and needs help!"

"When and Where did this happen?"

"I don't know, but I do know he's at the river right now," I said losing patience.

"Are you at the river, Winter?"

"No."

"How do you know your friend is at the river?"

I could feel Justin slipping away like sand through my fingers. I needed to get to him. Then I realized, with a start, that I could still feel him drawing me closer.

"Winter, are you still there?"

I closed my eyes, and reached out my mind to Justin's. The pull was weak but I could feel him. I needed to go right, continuing down Highway 19.

"Just send someone," I said and slammed the phone into its cradle.

They weren't going to send someone. I was on my own.

I got back into the car and headed northeast out of town, following the pull of Justin on my mind. The further down the road I got, the closer I got to Justin, the stronger the pull became, until I no longer had to even try to find his presence with my mind. I followed my connection with him down one dirt road, then another until I came to a dead end. And there, illuminated in my headlights, was a black Ford Explorer.

I pulled over onto the shoulder of the road, and killed the engine.

The sleet had stopped and the snow was now falling in big, fluffy globs. As I stepped out of the car, the first thing I noticed was how silent it was. The only sound was the crunch of my feet on the icy ground. The second thing I noticed was the cold. The temperature, which had been freezing, had dropped considerably. I was still wearing the black spandex dress and heels I'd worn to the club earlier, and I quickly reached for my coat, but the passenger seat was empty. I cursed under my breath, sending little puffs of steam rising into the air. I'd left my coat at Collin's house. I could still see it thrown over the arm of the chair in his living room. A fat lot of good it would do me there. I searched the glove box and found a pair of driving gloves and a scarf, which I put on.

Then with my mom's necklace clutched tightly in my gloved hand, I gritted my chattering teeth and headed into the forest, following the pull of Justin's mind. There was no light, and I could barely make out the shapes of the trees around me as I crunched through the rising snow. Each step sent a little more of the frozen drifts cascading into my shoes, which I was glad were closed toed. I couldn't image how my feet could be any colder, but logically I knew that if my toes were exposed they would be.

A blanket of snow, masked what little I could see of the forest floor, making it impossible to see tree roots or fallen limbs. I stumbled several times, but eventually made it to the rocky beach of the riverbank where, without the shadows of the trees, there was a bit more visibility.

There was no light to speak of, but the snow seemed to glow in contrast to everything else, and I could just make out the shadow of something lying on the ground by the river.

Justin.

I ran to him and grabbing his shoulder, rolling him onto his back. But it wasn't Justin, it was Amanda, or what was left of her. Her lips were blue, her cheeks were sunk in, and her skin was withered like a rotten apple. But her eyes—those emerald green eyes that I'd seen sparkle whenever she talked about Thomas—still held on to the hope and fear she had felt in her final moments. Amanda's eyes gazed heavenward as if pleading with God to take her and end her suffering.

I let go of her shoulder and scrambled away. I wanted to run from the corpse at my feet, to give into the insanity hovering at the periphery of my consciousness. But I couldn't, I needed to find Justin. Still, I could feel a scream building in my throat. But before I let it escape someone grabbed me roughly from behind, and covered my mouth with their hand. I thrashed about violently, trying to get out of the arms that were around me, but whoever was behind me was strong, and I couldn't get away from their iron grip. Finally, I bit down hard on the hand over my mouth, and they released me.

"Damn it, Winter," said the most wonderful voice in the world.

I turned around and threw my arms around Justin, nearly knocking him over.

"You're alive. I'm sorry about your hand. I didn't know it was you. Will it be okay?" I said, taking his hand in mine to examine it. His hand was bloody, his knuckles swollen. Then looking at his face, I noticed that his left eye was swollen most of the way shut, and there was dried blood under his nose. My little bite seemed like the least of his worries. "Justin, what happened?"

Justin drew me back into the shadows of the trees, and wrapped his coat around my shoulders. "I got into a fight at the club."

"Thanks," I said, pulling his coat tighter. "But Collin never hit you back. What happened to your face?"

"No, I got into another fight, after I left."

"Justin, what were you thinking? And why are you all the way out here?

"It was *him*," Justin said, as if that answered all of my questions. "Winter, did you drive your car here?"

"Yes," I whispered, "it's parked just beyond the trees."

"We need to leave *now*."

"What happened to Amanda?" I said, shuttering at the memory of her lifeless eyes, an image that would be forever burned into my retinas, and which would haunt me for years. "What is going on?"

"We'll talk about it later. Right now, we need to get out of here," Justin said, dragging me along behind him as he raced back into the woods.

We were about half way through the thicket, when a voice like oil on ice spoke behind us.

"Going so soon?"

Chapter 34

The man in front of me was attractive, with a medium build, dark brown hair, olive skin, and gray eyes. And I knew him. He worked at the theater and I'd seen him at the bowling ally. I'd always assumed he was Middle Eastern, but looking at him now, I wasn't so sure. His hair was too light and the shape of his nose and jaw line was wrong. Then there were his eyes. They looked kind of Asian, but not quite, and they looked out of place in his young face. His eyes looked ancient and ageless at the same time, as if they'd witnessed centuries of time, even though the boy before me didn't look much older than myself. And as foreign as his eyes seemed, there was still something familiar about them, that I couldn't place, and I found myself staring into them as if mesmerized.

"Winter, we meet at last."

"Do I know you?" I asked.

"No, but I know you. You live alone, and you occupy your time with boys you don't really care about, while you mother lies alone and helpless in a nursing home."

Despite the cold, I blushed. "You don't know anything about me."

"I know you are Paige's daughter, and that you are a Siren. How's that for not knowing anything?"

"I don't know what want, but just leave my mother out of it. She never did anything to you."

"Wrong again. She and I met many years ago and she stole something of mine. A very rare and valuable necklace, and I want it back."

I glanced down at my hand.

"Ah, I see you brought it with you."

"Winter, whatever you do, don't give it to him," Justin said, taking my hand in his, sending a reassuring warmth racing up my arm in the process.

The strange boy took his eyes off me for the first time, and glared at Justin. "You've served your purpose boy. I believe it's time for you to go."

Justin glared back coldly. "I don't think so."

The boy looked at Justin for a fraction of a second longer before he turned his gray eyes my way and his whole demeanor changed. "Winter, I need you to come with me," he said pleasantly.

When I didn't move, he dropped the pleasant act and gave Justin a look that reminded me of a snake about to strike, but Justin stared back coldly seemingly unfazed.

"Who are you? What do you want?"

The boy laughed a humorless laugh. "My name is Lamech. And as for what I want? I already told you. I want my necklace," Lamech paused and walked closer until he was standing right in front of me. "But what I didn't tell you is that I also want you."

"You're Lamech?" A chill crept down my spine. I wanted to run away screaming, but I was frozen with fear.

"I see you've heard of me. Good, then you know to be afraid. I took your friend over there, but you never came for her. So, I had to take your boyfriend here instead."

"Amanda?" I gasped, feeling the blood drain from my face.

"Was that her name? We never exchanged pleasantries. She was fun, though. I've always like redheads— they're fighters, and the ones that fight always taste better."

I felt bile rise into my throat. Taste?

"Come with me, Winter?"

"Never," I managed to choke out.

"Fine have it your way," he said.

Moving faster than humanly possible, Lamech reached over and touched one finger to the middle of Justin's forehead, and Justin slumped to the ground.

"He doesn't taste as good as the girl, but he's a fighter too," Lamech said, licking the finger he'd touched Justin with.

Justin's limp hand slipped out of my own, and suddenly I know with out a doubt that I was going to die. Strangely enough, that knowledge gave me the strength to do what I'd wanted to do from the moment I'd laid eyes on Lamech—run.

I turned and ran faster than I'd ever run before, but it was sleeting and I had tears in my eyes so I kept running into trees and getting caught in bushes. I'd meant to run to my car, but when I didn't reach it after a few minutes I realized I was lost. I wanted to keep running, to put as much distance between me and the monster behind me, but I was out of breath and need to get my bearings. In front of me I saw an evergreen tree with branches that hung so low they were almost touching the ground, and I dived under it.

I was shivering and my labored breaths were coming out in little white puffs. The temperature had really dropped since that afternoon, making me equally grateful and guilty that I had Justin's coat.

Justin.

I tried reaching out to him with my mind, but instead of feeling the reassuring presence of his mind, I felt something else—something dark.

A cold that cut deeper than the icy wind permeated the air around me, and somehow I knew I wasn't alone.

"Winter, I know you're out there," Lamech called from so nearby that I was afraid he could hear my heart pounding.

Then the cold around me shifted, pressing up against me like icy fingers, reaching out to my mind. Lamech was searching for me with more than just his eyes and ears, and I didn't know how long I had before he realized that he had found me, if h hadn't realized it already.

Desperately, I looked around for any kind of weapon, and found a large stick dangling in the branches above me. I grabbed it with both hands and pulled, but my hands slipped and it came crashing loudly to the forest floor. I held my breath. There was no way Lamech hadn't heard that. I probably had only seconds before he would find me. Looking down at my hands, I saw why the branch had slipped. I was still holding my mom's necklace. Whatever apprehension I had to wearing it didn't seem to matter anymore. I needed my hands free to defend myself, so I quickly slipped the necklace around my neck and picked up my stick.

I knew I needed to move. I couldn't trust my hiding spot any longer, so I crawled out and looked around, unsure which direction I should go. The trees seemed to go on forever in every direction.

I could still feel Lamech's mind grasping at my own. Those icy fingers were clawing their way into my brain. Then a voice as cold and slippery as his real one spoke in my mind.

"Winter, bring me the necklace."

I could feel the compulsion in the command, but I fought the urge to obey it, and stayed where I was. I felt violated. Was that what I did to people?

I instantly took back every mean thing I'd thought about Carrie. She was right. What I could do was vial and wrong, and I decided that if I ever made it out of this alive I was going to try harder to make up with her.

I had no idea where Lamech was so, holding my branch like a bat, I started creeping as quietly as possible in the direction I thought the car was. The sleet was still falling, and the sound helped cover any noise I made as I crunched through the snow and ice that had begun accumulating on the ground, but I knew that sound of the sleet would also make it harder to hear Lamech.

I paused listening for footfalls in the snow, but heard nothing. Then a twig snapped to my right and I bolted the other way, running blindly until I reached the riverbank. I was back where I'd started. I could still make out the form of Amanda's body, but it was already almost covered with a blanket of white. Justin was nowhere to be found.

Had he gotten away? I was trying once again to locate Justin with my mind, when Lamech stepped from the trees.

"There you are," he said as though we'd lost each other in the supermarket or something, as though my flight through the woods had meant nothing. "You will give me what I want."

I wanted to say something defiant. I wanted to tell him to go to hell, but I couldn't. I couldn't move. I'd never been so scared in all my life or so alone.

I'd never thought much about death or dying. Death had always seemed so far away. I'd never imagined it would come so soon. This was how my life would end.

I wondered how long it would take them to find my body, if anyone ever did. No one knew where I was. I had no family, hardly any friends. Would anyone even notice I was gone? I had no one but myself.

411

I looked at Lamech approaching and although my life seemed empty, I knew I wanted nothing more than to live it. If I was all I had, then I would do everything I could to survive. I was not going down without a fight.

Chapter 35

I gripped branch in my hand, holding it behind me, so that Lamech wouldn't see it. It wasn't much, but it would have to work. I would make it work. Lamech was walking casually toward me, his gray eyes locked on my own. I would only get one shot. I had to make it count.

Lamech smiled wickedly at me, and continued to approach. I could feel him trying to force his way into my mind again, but I shut him out, closing my mind off the same way I'd learned to do to keep from influencing others. But keeping him out was hard work, and I could already feel my strength wavering.

He was close enough now that I could see that his eyes weren't solid gray, but had a ring of lighter gray in the center. It was now or never, and I swung the branch as hard as I could at his head. The branch broke as it made contact, and without looking to see how Lamech was, I tossed what was left of the stick and ran. I ran as if my life depended on it, and I might have gotten away had not a wall of water risen from the stream and blocked my path.

I turned and it turned. I dodged and the watery wall blocked me again. I turned to run back the way I'd come, and before I knew it there was nothing but water in every direction. I was trapped in the eye of a ten-foot high vortex of water.

When Lamech parted the wall of water like a curtain and entered my watery prison, he'd dropped all pretenses of kindness or civility. A thin trail of blood fell from a gash on his forehead, and his eyes shown with hatred. As he drew closer, stalking me like an animal stalks it's prey, I wondered if it hurt to die.

414

I didn't want to hurt. I wanted to run or fight, but I suddenly felt dizzy and weak. I was losing feeling in my limbs, and my vision was clouding over. I was going to pass out, and sadly, part of me wondered if it wouldn't be easier that way.

"Winter, you need to fight it. Fight to stay awake."

In my state, I couldn't tell if I'd heard the voice with my ears or just my mind. But unlike Lamech's voice, this voice brought with it visions of warm sunshine and summer breezes, fresh baked bread and motherly hugs.

Then just like that, everything stopped. The wall behind me stood still. The falling snow hung suspended in the air, and Lamech had frozen arms extended only a foot from where I stood. His fingers were mere inches from bringing my death.

Without thinking, I backed away. Everything was frozen as if time had stopped, except me. For some reason, I could move.

Immediately I began searching for a way to escape, but the wall of water felt solid.

Winter, you must fight.

"You know what? I don't know why I'm hearing voices of people that clearly aren't there, maybe I've finally cracked and all of this is just in my head. But whoever you are, He just raised a freakin' watery tornado. Amanda's dead, maybe Justin too. That and I'm pretty sure the he's been around for centuries. I don't think there's much I can do against this guy."

It's true. He is very powerful. But you are gifted in ways you don't even realize yet, said the voice like sunshine in my mind.

416

"Who are you?"

I am Arianna, and I am a friend.

"And what makes you so sure I can do anything?"

The necklace you wear is cursed. The crystal was crafted for one purpose alone—to collect the soul of the whoever wears it. The fact that you are still standing is a testament of your strength.

I recalled those last few moments before time had stopped. The weakness. The feeling of fading.

That was the necklace, but you fought it.

"And why should I trust you?"

Winter, said a voice that cut to my heart. *Honey, you need to listen. I don't know how much time we have.*

"Mom?"

Paige is with me, as are other who have worn the necklace and succumbed to its darkness.

I thought of all the times I'd held the necklace and felt my mother's presence, and knew it was true.

"Okay, let's say I believe you. What is it you want me to do? I mean, why can't you do something?"

We have no power to do anything. We are bound.

"Then how'd you stop time like this," I asked looking around at the surreal scene around me. Lamech's gray eyes were focused on me, and once again I got that feeling like I'd seen them somewhere else, but then the moment was gone.

We didn't. You did.

The moment she said it, time stared again. The ice pellets hovering in the air crashed down with so much force they stung. Lamech was on me in a flash, his hands on the sides of my head. I didn't really believe that it had been me who has stopped time, but I sure tried to do it again as I struggled to get out of Lamech's grip.

"Help! What do I do?" I screamed out in my mind.

He lives by feeding on the chi or life-force of other's. Every time he steals someone's chi, he gets a piece of their soul. The more life-force he takes from them, the bigger chunk of their soul he possesses. He has no soul of his own, so in order to live he must fill that void with the souls of others.

Despite the cold, Lamech's hands on my head felt hot, and there was a searing pain behind my temples. I could feel something inside of me trying to break free, as he tried to collect my soul.

"That's what he did to Amanda, and to Justin, and what he's trying to do to me. Is Justin dead then?" I asked silently.

That depends on how much chi he took. We all have a certain amount of energy within us, and like blood, it is renewed regularly. Like with blood, if you lose a little you can recover, but lose too much and it's deadly.

"But he can do that by touching them, so what does he need the necklace for?" I asked.

He made the necklace to capture one soul in particular—the soul of an angel. To take her soul the way he takes others would have killed him, like light killing a shadow. So he found another way to take it. If he gets the necklace, and finds a way to use it, he will be immortal.

"But can't he already live forever?"

Right now, his life has been prolonged as long as he steals life from others, but he can still die. However, if he steals the soul of an angel he would never die. There would be no stopping him.

"So how do I kill him?"

You must compel him to release the souls and parts of souls he has taken.

I wasn't sure how I was supposed to do that, but I decided to mimic what Lamech had done by putting my hands on his head. I began pushing with my mind, telling him to release the souls, but it was like pushing against a brick wall.

"He's too strong. I can't get into his head."

Then you will have to weaken him. You need to sing.

"Okay, but what do I sing? I don't think I know any songs like that."

There is a song my mother taught me long ago that should work. Sing with me, Arianna said.

Then she began to sing a song so beautiful no words could describe it, but my mind still tried. It was the sound of dawn breaking, or the white-hot flash of lightning. It was the sound you hear when the clouds finally part and let the sun shine through on a rainy day.

Obediently, I sang, and immediately a burning started in my throat. As I continued to sing, the burning spread through my body, and into my extremities. It wasn't until it reached the tips of my finger that I realized that what was raging through my body was light. As I sang, light was filling my being, coursing through my body, and burning everything in its wake. I was glowing, bathing the entire area in a warm golden light.

Lamech screamed as though he'd stuck his hands inside a furnace, but didn't seem able to let go. Then the whirlpool came crashing down around us, nearly knocking me over. It was so cold it took my breath away, but somehow, I managed to keep singing.

The song you sing is light itself. He cannot survive in the light, already he has begun to weaken. Now use your gift. Compel him to release them.

While I sang, I pushed again at his mind, and this time I got through.

"Release them, I compel thee. Send them home, I command thee."

I wasn't sure where the words had come from, but somehow I knew they were right. And as I sent the thought, I knew I'd never sent a message more powerful.

Lamech winced as the command hit home.

Then I felt them. The souls Lamech has stolen began rushing through my fingers and up my arms. It was terrifying how amazing it felt, as the imprisoned souls of his victims filled me.

"What's happening?"

You've opened up some sort of conduit.

"What do I do?"

Just keep singing.

"But they're not being freed. They're just going into me."

Then free them.

For a moment, I didn't want to. I can't even describe what a rush I felt as they poured into me. But as good as it felt, what held me mesmerized was that I could feel each and every one of them. To my surprise not all of them were Sirens. In fact, most of them were just girls who had been in the wrong place at the wrong time. But even though their lives had ended I could still feel their feelings, see their memories. It was as if in that moment, I'd lived a thousand different lives. Lamech had been doing this for a very long time.

I looked at Lamech, and was shocked to see that his once youthful face now creased and there was gray in his hair. He'd aged more than twenty years and he continued to age before my eyes, as the life sustaining energy was drained from his body

It was like watching one of those time progression movies about the growth of mold, only with a person. Vaguely I wondered if my appearance had changed. Did I look younger? More beautiful? Were my eyes ageless the way that Lamech's had been?

In that moment, I was intoxicated by the power of it all, but then I looked into those familiar gray eyes, and the look he was giving me was almost triumphant. He knew. Was this how he felt every time he preyed on those weaker than him? Did he get this kind of rush every time he fed?

It was then that I remembered why I was there, and all doubt left me. I had to put them to rest. I was ready.

Letting them go was like loosing my grip on a bird caged in my hands. As soon as the decision was made thin golden wisps of light began rising from my skin like steam.

"Are those what I think they are?" I asked.

Those are the souls of his victims.

I watched in awe as the ethereal lights filled the air around Lamech and me before soaring into the sky above us and out of sight. They were beautiful.

"Where are they going?"

The whole ones will go on to the next life, while the partial ones will go looking for their other half. Broken souls can't enter heaven, so for all of those that he didn't kill, when they did die, what was left of their souls remained on earth as shades. Now they can finally be at rest.

As I continued to sing, a gold strand of light stopped in front of my face and reached out to me before ascending into heaven. It was Amanda.

She's at peace now, Arianna said.

"What about you?"

Though the souls of Lamech's victims were now being released, Arianna, my mother, and the others were still trapped in the crystal.

We are with you as long as you wish us to be, said a chorus of voices.

It was comforting to know that I wasn't alone. I felt a surge of pride for these Sirens who were willing to fight with me, but they had suffered enough.

"I release you."

I could feel their gratitude as they began rising into the heavens.

Winter, I'm proud of you, and I love you, my mom said.

With tears running down my cheeks I said, "*I love you too, Mom.*"

Good-bye, sweetheart.

"*Good-bye, Mom.*"

Then she was gone.

"*Is she dead?*" I asked Arianna.

I don't know, Arianna said. *Her body is still alive, so perhaps not.*

"*What about you?*"

I must be going soon, too. My soul is still in pieces, and I go to find them, but I will be back when you need me.

"*Good luck.*"

Then she left and I was alone.

Lamech was no more than a skeleton now, his skin like dry parchment, and the look he was giving me was pure hatred, but I kept singing. He had managed to pull his hands from my head, but didn't have the strength to step out of my grip. His hands and forehead were black and charred where he had been touching me, and he could no longer stand to look at the light radiating from my body.

He was weak, but so was I. My throat felt like sandpaper, and my insides felt like the desert. The light I was singing into existence was burning up my insides, and I wasn't sure how much longer I would make it, but I kept singing.

"RELEASE THEM ALL!"

I put all the power I could behind the words, but I was weak, and I wasn't sure if the thought had even escaped my own mind.

But then a few more wisps of light rose into the air, and the skin on his emaciated scalp stretched tighter, before breaking apart and exposing his skull underneath.

I was going to kill him.

The thought was both nauseating and relieving. It would be over soon, if I could just hold out a little longer.

Then in what I believe were his final moments he turned to face me, and suddenly I knew why his eyes were so familiar. I'd seen them before in an old photograph that had been snatched away before I'd really even gotten to look at it. And I saw them stare back at me every time I looked in the mirror.

"Dad?"

The realization was like a punch in the stomach, and it was a second before I realized that I had stopped singing.

In that moment of startled silence, Lamech gave me a dangerous smile and reached out one charred, brittle finger to my forehead.

The last thought I had before everything went black was how pretty the sunrise looked as it cut through the skeletal trees around me.

Chapter 36

In the darkness, there was a voice.

Winter, you need to wake up now.

Justin?

You did it. You stopped him.

I couldn't kill him. Even though he killed Amanda, and tried to kill you, I just couldn't do it.

But you kept him from getting what he wanted.

Justin, I'm sorry I didn't listen to you.

I don't blame you. I love you. But you need to wake up.

I wanted to escape back into the comfort of nothingness, but a voice was calling to me, and I drifted toward it.

I was in a bed, the covers pulled up to my chest. There was a white tile ceiling above me, and someone was holding my hand.

"Justin?"

I looked over and saw my mother.

"Hey, honey. Welcome back."

"Mom? Mom!"

"Oh, baby, it's okay, I'm here," my mom reached over and wiped my cheeks, and I realized I was crying.

"Where am I? What happened?"

"You're in the hospital, and that's what everyone is waiting to ask you."

"What do you mean? Who?"

"The police found you lying unconscious by the river five days ago, next to Amanda's body."

"Where'd Justin go?"

433

"We'll talk about Justin later. Right now, you need your rest." I could tell my mom was trying to sound cheerful, but her voice caught when she said Justin's name, and I knew something was wrong.

I heard my heart monitor go crazy. "What aren't you telling me?"

"Honey, he's missing. He hasn't been seen since the night the police found you."

Made in the USA
Columbia, SC
20 August 2017